Pigeon

Alys Conran

Parthian, Cardigan SA43 1ED
www.parthianbooks.com
First published in 2016
© Alys Conran 2016
ISBN 978-1-910901-23-6
Editor: Richard Davies
Cover design by Robert Harries
Typeset by Elaine Sharples
Printed and bound by Printed in EU by Pulsio SARL
Published with the financial support of the Welsh Books Council
British Library Cataloguing in Publication Data
A cataloguing record for this book is available from the British Library.

i Mam
who resuscitated this book with tears

'Look up pigeon in your good field guide, if you have one. You will probably find that the pigeon does not exist. The most obvious bird in the country doesn't even rate a mention. There seems to be a conspiracy of silence about the pigeon, as if pigeons were an embarassment to birdwatchers – as if pigeons were an embarassment to proper birds. Pigeons, however, exist. There they are, eating McDonald's chips at railway stations, hanging about on precipitous ledges above the hooting streets, pursuing their love lives with unbridled enthusiasm around the ankles of pedestrians. Try telling them they are not proper birds.'

Simon Barnes *The Bad Birdwatcher's Companion, or a personal introduction to Britain's 50 most obvious birds*

'Nor shall I waste my time on pigeons, or doves as they are sometimes called, though some people seem to regard them as a fit subject for literature. To me pigeons mean just about nothing.'

Gunter Grass *The Tin Drum*

1

Gwyn's Ice Creams come in a pink and yellow van, stickers and posters peeling from the windows. Chugging away beyond a curtain of mountain and through bloom of cloud, the van clambers the to and fro road up the hillside every Saturday and Sunday afternoon. Every weekend of the year it stutters up, choking, and spitting exhaust fumes, but stubborn against the grey of the hill and the town. Whining tunes come from Gwyn's van as it rattles up the hill, set against the drone and moan of the grumbling engine.

The van's tunes are sweet on my tongue. Music from the past 200 years all put into that bell-like warble that means ice cream and tickles kids from their houses like the pied piper. Somehow the reel's connected to the accelerator, so that the tune deepens, slows with the road, and then the tape speeds on at a trot and a gallop whenever the van accelerates, desperately, against the steep hill.

"IIIII shhhhhhoooooouuuuuuulllllllddddddddd beeeeee soo luuckky lucky lcky lki i shd b so lcki in luv," says the tape.

Heaven.

My mouth waters. As Pigeon and me run, my shoes are still undone and Pigeon's too small school trousers, which he's wearing although it's Sunday, make his steps shorter like in a three-legged race. We race anyway, over fences, between the jumble of houses that cluster on the hillside. With snotty noses, with mouths catching at the air like fish out of water, we arrive at the slot in the van. Gwyn's round brown and red face looks out, smiling. We bend to pant, our breath steaming all round us, white in the frosty air. We bend to breathe, our hands on our knees, backs rounded to the clouds, like that guy off the Olympics, the fastest runner in the world.

Gwyn's looking down at us through the slot. He has thick, bristly black eyebrows and little dark blue eyes. He has a belly like a pot. Gwyn's skin's different to mine or Pigeon's. Gwyn's skin is tanned and like oiled leather. On his head there's some black hair he brushes over his bald patch. This hair always ends up sticking straight up: like a by-mistake mohican. He has black hairs all up his arms too and Gwyn has a hairy face. Not long hair, just bristly like my dad's was. Gwyn's voice is bristly too. And he has what Efa calls a stutter, where there's a blank space where your word should be, and your whole body stops.

"Iawn, b b bois?" he asks us.

Together Pigeon and me breathe "Iawn" back, although everyone knows I'm not a boi, any more than Pigeon is a prissy hogan – but I quite like being called a boi by Gwyn.

"B b be 'dach chi isio heddiw 'ta?" Gwyn's question goes up at the end, really high, as high as here; but we still haven't decided. Because last week I had one of the chocolate ones with the creamy outside and Pigeon had one of those thin orangey things and we said we'd swap this week but I don't really want to cause the chocolate one is my favourite and I'm hoping Pigeon agrees but he hasn't said so yet so I'm on the edge of going right ahead and having something else completely but I wouldn't want to make the wrong choice. Pigeon's my best friend.

Waiting, Gwyn, to keep talking, says "Tywydd braf", and

2

he grins. We grin back because this is no more fine weather than Pigeon is a hogan, or I'm a boi, or Gwyn's van's a BMW or we're all Colin Jackson doing the hurdles.

The weather's come in again; it sits all over the hill and the clouds are blowing up now like a balloon water bomb and they have a grey colour that's almost dark blue, so you know it'll rain forever.

In the end of thinking I have the long orange thing and Pigeon has the chocolate one like we decided last week. See? Pigeon and me, we're like *this*.

We're walking back between the houses, our heads full of thinking like televisions, and our feet scraping along the ground, with our shoelaces left behind. And I lick it.

"Gwyn's a gypsy," Pigeon says.

I look at him. I'm not quite sure what that means. "He's a gyppo," says Pigeon. Ah.

It's cos of Gwyn telling on Pigeon. Telling Pigeon's stepdad about the lolly Pigeon stole. How Pigeon ran off without paying, his coat and his shoelaces trailing and bouncing as if they were running from Gwyn too. Pigeon got a black eye for that. Pigeon hates Gwyn cos all the other kids saw. Saw what happened when Gwyn shouted that he'd tell his 'dad', how Pigeon came running back and then followed Gwyn all the way begging him please not to, not to tell. The kids at school say Pigeon was crying, although that isn't true, is it? I can't imagine it. It was days before anyone saw him after that, and when he came out again, he had that black eye.

"Ma' Gwyn yn od," says Pigeon.

And that's it forever after that. Gwyn is 'od', funny, strange. It'd never occurred to us before. And that's what started this whole thing off, licking those ice creams, thinking, and then that idea of Pigeon's: Gwyn = Od.

3

2

This morning, before the ice creams, as he sat alone in his shed bedroom, Pigeon had been able to see his new sister Cher getting ready for school in his old room. He didn't watch, but he could see. Pigeon knelt on his bed. The shadow from the house fell on the shed's window, and the other window, in the house, with Cher in it, made its impression on Pigeon and the shed.

Cher did up her blouse, buttoning all the way up the front. The cool blue of the shirt, it was so gentle over her soft skin. Cher's face, serious, quiet and serious, just like Cher's face always is.

She started combing her hair out, its sleek and lithe mass, heavy down her back. She pulled it all back off her face into a tight ponytail, brushing and brushing so that all the strands were streamlined in the same direction, and it looked smooth, her hair, like a slow and wide river, or like the satin of a ball gown.

Pigeon's mam came, making her way down from the kitchen. And she had the tray in her white hands. His mam brought their breakfast down to the shed. And this was the best part of the day. His mam though, always looked tired, and perhaps not very well.

They sat on the bed, Pigeon and his mam, with the cereal

and the tea. Pigeon drank black tea, his mam white. The air was cold, so that the tea lifted from the cup in streaks of steam. His mam had a blue mark on her face again, blue and yellow, like a wet sunset. This one was because there were other men looking at her. And He saw them. They were looking because she's beautiful. But He said it was because she was 'asking for it'. Which she wasn't. She'd never ask for anything at all.

Pigeon's mam ruffled his hair, until it all stuck up, and Pigeon, Pigeon almost smiled then, before she picked up the tray and went to the house.

As she went, she told Pigeon in her cracked, soft voice to "Hurry now, love. Get dressed", and, although it was Sunday, she told him to get on off to school, as if it was a dream, a hope, and not telling him what to do, and it was as if her voice was getting lost in the air on the way to his ears.

Pigeon pulled on his grey school trousers, and his only black shoes, his only white shirt and his only green jumper. And he hated and hated the way the ugly clothes felt when he pushed his arms through into them, and how the clothes were scraping and pulling at him, trying to skin him alive. And, without going to the house, so that He didn't see him, or Cher either, with her pretty smooth hair, her perfect clothes and her sorry eyes, Pigeon went on, pretended to his mam to be going to school, to the tit-for-tat-tattletale school where, between Monday and Friday, he kept his head down, right down under the radar.

Pigeon went over the wall, and down the path that was like a snake by the wood as it followed the river as that went down with the weight of the rain and the grey sky and the hill. And then Pigeon stopped. Sat. What to do with an empty Sunday? And with a half-empty mother too?

She appeared. It was Iola, come out of the wood like a genie, small with a pot belly over her skirt, knees as always covered in bruises and grazes, shoes undone, hair so light it's almost white. Beckoning.

Pigeon took a quick look up the path in case of his mam, and then ran after Iola through the wood and back up the hill again into the grey, into the grey full of purple and orange stories that go on and on and on

They ran together to Iola's house, to where there was a real kitchen, a real home, and as the van started its meandering songs up the road, Efa and Iola danced in the kitchen, and, smiling a little too brightly, Efa put two fifty p's in Iola's white palm.

Heaven.

At the van, Iola and Pigeon, their breath steamy in the cold January air, order one chocolate thing, and one orangey thing, cos, like Pigeon tells Iola, they're "saff", and it's good they're safe, cause that chocolate one, it's delicious.

But Pigeon stares at Gwyn's hands as he hands Iola the ice-creams. He stares at Gwyn's man's hands. And he hates him.

Gwyn is growing in Pigeon's mind. He grows and is altered and bent out of shape. Pigeon would give him horns, would have him turn rotten inside. Pigeon fires up so much anger about Gwyn, that he can still smell him, long after leaving the van, and long after leaving Iola to her home, her chores, her regular life.

3

The next bit is when I'm on Pigeon's bed in the shed. I'm reading a comic, lying, bol down, and Pigeon is bol up, his legs stretching up the shed wall. Ryan Giggs is looking down at us from the poster, looking good, but next to me, Pigeon's ignoring Ryan and looking at his wood ceiling, where the blue-tack holds part of an old mobile: half an aeroplane and a crumbly cloud. I just read my comic, and I'm almost there, at the end, when "Murdyryr! Dyna be 'di o: murdyryr!"

I'm looking up from my comic, a bit surprised. We've thought of a few things: kiddie fiddler, woman in a man's body, a ghost, but Pigeon's never got quite this far. Murderer… It feels like a big word to say, echoing between the four walls of Pigeon's small room like trying on Efa's big shoes.

Now Pigeon's my best friend, but Pigeon keeps cut-outs of all sorts of things. He'll like something, so he'll cut it out. Recipes, even though he can't cook, bits and pieces of Cher's comics, someone's marked homework, his mam's birthday card, tickets, bits of receipts. He keeps them all under his bed in the shed, like a hamster making a nest. Paper isn't the only thing Pigeon keeps, he also keeps money, and he keeps information: names, numbers, jobs, secrets, lies, lined up in his head like a dictionary with the town and the whole world in. This isn't quite a normal thing, but Pigeon's my best friend, and anyway he hardly ever talks about all the information he has in his head, and at school they don't know. They don't know what he does all day when he's not there. They don't really care. And anyway he'll make a note if they ask. Like the one he made for me.

And with the note you can spend all day free. You can spend the day outside, in the wood or up in the old quarries, sitting, making a fire and laughing and making stories out of everything. With Pigeon everything is bright and big and better than you'd think it was. It's all freed up when me and Pigeon don't bother with school. You can stay out all day, until half past three. At half past three me and Pigeon had come back to the shed, and we'd eaten the crackerbreads he'd got stashed under the bed. Sometimes there are cigarettes there, but he hasn't got any today. Today is a thinking day.

There's a sound at the door of the shed. Someone trying to get in. Pigeon's sister, who's called Cher, after Cher, except actually she's Cheryl. Cher is new. Which is amazing, that you can have a new sister, new mother excetera. I'd like a new sister or a mother too, except that mine'd smell new and nice, not like Cher, who, Pigeon says, smells like rotten fish.

Cher is good at school, better than me, and a lot better than Pigeon. She's good at school and she goes every day, and only comes back here when it's over, like now. Cher has a room in the house, not like Pigeon. Cher has long brown hair and brown eyes, which are very pretty and soft like feathers and cushions and cotton wool. Cher likes doing cartwheels, on the tarmac at school her legs go all round in the air and she looks like a wheel. But Cher only speaks English. English is sludgy.

8

"PIJIN! Just cause you've got stuck in the shed doesn't mean it's my fault!"

"I'm not sayin it is, just saying you can't come in. Anyway, Cher, keep your knickers on and stop bein' so loud else your dad's going to hear us, an we'll be dead."

"I'll only be quiet if you open the door."

"No."

"Why?"

"Cause"

"Why?"

"Shush ... just cause, Cher. Just cause."

"Why, Pijin?"

"Piss off, Cher!"

"No."

"Just stay there an be quiet then okay?"

Silence

"Why is she allowed in an I'm not?"

"Cause we're mates."

"We can be mates too."

"Don't wanoo."

"WHY?"

"Cause."

"Why really?"

"Cause you smell bad, an anyway I just don't."

"Fine, don't care anyway."

"Okay, me either."

"You goin?"

"No... Pijin..."

"What?"

"Jew really think Gwyn's a murdrer?"

"Probly."

"Why?"

"Dunno – I can smell it."

"Whas it smell like?"

"Blood."

"Yuck."

"Yeh."

"So what're you going to do about it?"

"Get im."

"O... How?"

"Dunno yet."

"Can *I* help?"

"Nope."

"Why?"

"Cause."

"C'mon Pijin!"

"No way. Shut up."

"Pijin…"

"Piss off Cher!"

"Can I stay here though? Just to listen,"

"Aright … but don't shout."

"Ok"

"Pijin,"

"What?"

"What, Cher, spit it out."

"Pijin … I'm sorry about what He did … I'm sorry about what dad did, Pijin."

"Pijin"

"Pijin?"

"Pijin?"

"Just shut up Cher okay?

...just shut up."

I can tell Cher hates me cos she looks at me with big eyes that are sometimes crying. In here, in the dark under the covers, Pigeon holds a torch up to his chin and tells horrible stories to me about Gwyn and all his victims. The duvet glows with the light of the torch.

"Ar noson dywyll," begins Pigeon.

On a dark, dark night.

Gwyn is a psycho and kiddy fiddler, knife carrier, mask wearer, pain-lover, torturer, and all the other things that come from those programmes on the TV that Pigeon watches, and I don't because of Efa, and which make him speak English like cowboys and say things like "Rho dy hands up or I'll shoot!" and "Rhedeg i ffwrdd on the count of three, neu dwi mynd i make mincemeat of you!"

Gwyn makes such a good bad guy that sometimes Pigeon even freaks himself out, turns pale under the duvet and goes quiet, like a path that gets lost up a grey hill. He snaps at me like an alligator when I laugh cos he's scared.

He's been collecting the evidence against Gwyn, spying on the van, asking for a receipt when he gets an orangey thing, trying to find out where Gwyn lives, and scratching bits of dirt from the van's wheels to put into little sandwich bags to bring home. Pigeon's even got an old magnifying glass, stole it from my house, but Efa'll not notice, and he's borrowed a microscope from school, carrying it all the way up the hill and stashing it in the shed.

"Wha you going to do with tha?" Cher catches Pigeon and me on the way into the shed with it.

"Anna lice it," says Pigeon.

"Snot anna lice, stewpit, it's analyse."

But Pigeon just lets his shoulders go up and down like he doesn't care and gets on with analysing the yellow juice that's what's left over from his ice lolly.

Pigeon and me suspect Gwyn of a lot of things: poisoning, fraud, drug dealing and spying. We can't be sure yet, even with the all the facts lined up on the duvet: the evidence, documentary evidence, eggsybit 1. 2. 3. Even with these we can't be sure. But Gwyn's dangerous; Pigeon's sure, and I'm sure too, saying 'hmm' and 'aaahhhh' at all the eggsybits. And Cher listens from outside. She listens to the English in between, and now she's getting more and more of the other words that are all wrapped round it. And Cher one hundred per cent believes it all in a funny real kind of a way.

"Ma Gwyn yn od," I tell Efa, at home.

"Gwyn is a Psycho, a Kiddie Fiddler, a Mask Wearer and a Torturer," I tell Efa, saying the words like prizes.

"Don't talk like that, Iola," Efa says back, stirring the hippy soup in the kitchen. "Paid a deud petha fel'na." And then she says it, what she always says, says: Be Careful With Pigeon, Iola. Iola Be Careful With That Boy Pigeon.

Although she likes him.

I can tell Efa likes Pigeon cos she sits at the kitchen table and gets him to read her bits from the newspaper. Every time he reads a bit, Efa gives him a chocolate. And I'd bet Pigeon likes Efa too, cos he looks at Efa like she's some kind of an alien cos of all her beads and hippy smells and skirts. And I feel funny cos it isn't like as if Efa cares about the newspaper. She's just getting Pigeon to read, to see if she can, and Pigeon knows it. I'm black blue inside with the two of them making friends, like as if Efa's his mother or something, and it's like something inside me's going bad, before it's even begun.

4

Pigeon scuffs around the town, thinking of Gwyn, until the thoughts turn so smudged they're black like something burnt and ruined. When that happens, Pigeon starts peering in through people's windows, looking for light. He's a scavenger, a scavenger for comfort. Day to day to day, Pigeon drags his feet around his pebble-dashed kingdom. Non-descript, gloomy, at the wrong end of nowhere. Perhaps.

But below the grey domain of this hill, the patchwork fields stretch their expanse of emerald down, sloping to a silver sea of torn paper waves. And above, above the hill, there are the crouching mountains, with their lakes, like broken mirrors wedged between valleys, and along the tops of the plaited ridges there's that trembling, pencil-line horizon. It's worth a second look. Just briefly.

So here, here's Pigeon again. Here, grey. Just a sketch the boy. His face is sallow. There's a snarl at his lips, and his shoulders are delicate as eggshells. Pigeon, here on the hill, wanders the pebble-dash, pebbled ash, scuffing his feet up the hill, and then up between the houses.

Pigeon goes right up to the top of the hill. To where you can sit and look down at the town all spread out like a handkerchief. Pigeon spits at it. He can spit a long way now, but still, the gob of spit lands on the grass just below him, and the town is still there. Pigeon sits on the hill, legs crossed, watching the day turning slowly. When his legs are cold through the school trousers, Pigeon stands, shakes out his legs and starts back down, for the town, the houses in their higgledey rows. He walks back into it. Into the pattern of the town, and scuffs along the streets between the shapes of the houses.

He stops at one that's off balance. It's skiw wiff. Crooked. Bits and pieces of it shoot out in all directions, like a peculiar, mangled space ship. It's Pigeon's house. Outside is Pigeon's shed. That's Pigeon's hole.

Pigeon avoids the house, and goes straight round to his shed.

Back in the good days the house was chaotic, a tangle of words and arguments, and conversations even, and even fun.

Like this very particular day, back then, in the house, in spring. It was her birthday, and Pigeon's mam had put on such a beautiful dress, and, in the dress, she was spinning and spinning in the kitchen, so that the pretty flowers on the dress streaked through the air, and a dish was knocked off the draining board by the spinning flowers on the dress. And that day she just laughed, that day, and her laugh, it was easy, like a soft breeze. So pretty, Pigeon's mam, like a ghost, but pretty.

Pigeon can remember that day. Pigeon can still remember, and he tells his mam about it, sitting on his bed in the shed in the falling night this Sunday. And she's quiet, but she strokes his hair as he lies his head on her lap, as he talks. And her hands are soft as feathers, so that Pigeon doesn't know if they're

15

there at all. Her hands are like fairies and so is she, so that she might disappear, fade, be taken somewhere else. Pigeon smiles at her, to keep her with him, and her hands stroking his hair feel a little more real, on the bed in the almost dark.

Pigeon keeps his mam there, and he's important, holding her hand now on the bed, smiling at her, and telling her about his day. And she asks him no questions. And he talks on and on, although she looks as if she doesn't understand, her grey look; the words evaporating away into the cloud of her eyes.

"At the bottom of the river there's a load of junk, Mam," he tells her in Welsh, painting a picture of what he's seen, the rubbish, the tipped, thrown-away toys and belongings clogging the river at the bottom of the hill, the things people have thrown away, as if they want nothing now, as if they need nothing.

Does she understand? Is she interested in him?

There are never any questions, never any explanations, but, as he talks, Pigeon feels her hand grow heavier in his, so he keeps talking until she kisses his hair, and it's time for bed.

Before He came, Pigeon's mam was a seamstress. She sewed, at home. She made dresses for other people. But now see the dresses, as they still hang in the dark lounge under plastic coats, like bodies, strangled. Underneath the plastic there are all the colours in the world: shiny, flat, soft, shimmery, see through, materials called beautiful names, chiffon, silk, satin. And Pigeon expected to see pretty girls in the dresses. Beautiful. But the ones who came to get them were always ugly, and never as pretty as his mam. No, never as pretty as she when she laughed. (Although it wasn't now so very often that she laughed.)

Before He came Pigeon was inside. Pigeon's bedroom was

upstairs before He came. He came bringing Cher and silence, and the shed.

When He first moved in, they got off to a bad start. Pigeon was sitting on the sofa, or rather he was draped over the sofa, lording over the room, his trainers kicked off, and strewn on the floor. He was reading a book. It was a book about aeroplanes. Back then that was what Pigeon liked, aeroplanes. Back then.

Pigeon's mam brought Him round.

At that time she still went out, at that freewheeling time still went for the shopping of her own free will, still took a bus into town. She had a friend, who she met once a week, to exchange dress patterns, have a cup of tea, talk.

Talk. Back then she did that too. Usually when she returned to the house, she'd come in through the back door. Like a lot of people they left the front door 'for visitors' although they never had any, and the ones they did, like Iola, came round the back too. So, usually, the front door was almost just a wall. Something that never moved, never opened. Pigeon sat upright when he heard a key turning in the front door that day. You knew it was trouble when it was the front. The police, the social worker, some kids playing pranks.

It took her a while to get her key into the lock, and even longer to turn it. Pigeon could hear her apologising, so there was someone there with her.

"I'm sorry. Oh, sorry," she said, fumbling with the key.

Then there was a man's voice saying "I'll do it. I'll do it."

And then Pigeon got to his feet, walked down the hall, and wrenched the door open, making the first crack in the door as he yanked it.

"O," she said.

"Oh," said the man.

"O," said Pigeon.

"Pigeon this is Adrian," she said in English

"Hi."

"What's your name again, son?"

Pigeon didn't like the way 'son' sounded.

"Pigeon."

"Hi Pigeon," He said. And when He smiled you didn't believe it.

"Can we come in, Pigeon?" asked his mam in English, smiling, motioning gently to the hallway he was blocking.

Pigeon wanted to say no. He wanted to say this is my house, no you can't. But he stepped back against the wall and let them pass.

The man went down the hallway making comments as if he was looking to buy the house.

"Nice location isn't it? Feels like heaven up here after the city. Clean air. Green views. I could do this. If there was work here, I could do this."

"What does He do?" Pigeon asked his mam. Walking behind them to the lounge.

"Why don't you ask me yourself, son?"

"What do you do?" Pigeon said without smiling.

"I work on the docks."

Pigeon didn't know what that meant, so he said nothing.

"How old are you, son?"

Pigeon shrugged.

"You'll be a bit younger than my daughter Cheryl I think. You'll like her. She's a lovely girl."

Pigeon didn't say anything.

He went back and sat on the sofa, he turned the TV on, loud.

"Pigeon," said his mam, and sighed a small, powerless sigh.

When Pigeon looked up at Him he was looking back at Pigeon, frowning. Pigeon turned the TV up two points, looked at the man, looked away and smiled to himself. You didn't let someone in through the front door, and then make them feel at home. And anyway Pigeon didn't like the way the man was looking all round the house, and saying "Nice light room this. This one could do with a splash of paint, love." He called Pigeon's mam 'love', but his voice sounded uncomfortable around the word. His hands were big, Pigeon had noticed that. They were the hands of a man who liked to limit things.

He started coming at weekends. He'd be sitting in the living room, on the sofa, when Pigeon came home. He'd be watching a programme He wanted to watch. He'd be getting Pigeon's mam to make Him dinner. He'd be telling them all things about the world. He'd not be listening to Pigeon's mam, nor leaving her space for an answer.

"Africa's a lost cause," He said, watching the black children with the empty eyes and round bellies. "It's just a useless country." He said.

"It's not a country," Pigeon said. "It's a continent."

"Same difference."

"No. There's lots of countries in it. Chad, Tanzania, South Africa." He'd got that from Iola's big geography book.

But He just looked at Pigeon, just looked at him.

What Pigeon didn't like was how his mam went so quiet when He was around. She was nervous. He made her feel as if everything was wrong. You could see it. It wasn't that He said so exactly. But He was always checking everything.

He checked the clothes she'd washed and ironed. Looking at each one for marks or creases. "Okaaaay. Okaaaaay," He said, going through the pile. When she brought out dinner, He'd look at his plate and just say, "Oh. I see."

"What's wrong?" she'd ask in that voice like a kid's.

"No, darling. Nothing." Then He'd hesitate, then hold her hand, look into her eyes, as if she knew nothing. "You just don't put parsnips with potatoes," he'd say. Or, "Too much gravy."

And then she'd say it. She'd always say it. "Sorry," she'd say. "Sorry."

You had to never say that word. It was like when a dog lies on its back, legs in the air, letting another dog growl over it. Sorry. She kept saying it. Sorry. And she got quieter and quieter, and He, He started to take her over.

Then He brought Cher for a weekend. Cher. She arrived through the front door too.

"Pigeon, can you carry Cher's case?" had been the first question. It was a pink suitcase. Cher was stood there, in a perfect blue dress. She looked like she'd come to the wrong house. Pigeon could see something else in her eyes. Fear. Pigeon took the case. Took it up to 'her' room.

His mam had asked him yesterday.

"Pigeon, we've only two bedrooms, and it's summer so, Adrian was wondering, if you'd mind us setting you up with a bed in the shed just for this weekend, so Cher can have her own room."

So this was the way it was going to be. Pigeon took his posters out to the shed straight away, his mobile of aeroplanes, all his clothes. It was better, when people tried to do something to you, to do it yourself, and worse. At school, when they tried to hit him, Pigeon'd punch himself in the eye, to stop them. They'd stare at Pigeon like there was something wrong with him. And now this was the same. People called it 'cutting off your nose to spite your face', but it put you back in the middle of things, so it was worth it. Even during the week Pigeon wouldn't go back to the house.

"You want me back? You'll have to get rid of Him," he'd say when his mam begged him. Why didn't she? Why didn't she? That was his mam, she couldn't make decisions on her own. She couldn't say no to anyone, or anything. But he loved her. Pigeon loved her.

She couldn't say no to getting married. In the photo on the mantelpiece, she wears a dress she made for someone else. She had to take it in. She's beautiful in it. But slight and pale. He stands behind her, holding her shoulders as if she's a steering wheel. In the photograph you can see that his hands are heavy. She looks at the camera, her eyes making blank lenses back.

Then He lost his job. They lost their house in Liverpool, and they turned up, at the front door, on a Tuesday in October. And after that it was all watching the house from the shed. It was all not being part of the house. It was all setting up a whole world in the shed. Making it into something big.

So tonight Pigeon's shed's like the moon. It keeps at a prudent distance. Pigeon's shed sits, watching from the edge of the garden, bent low and afraid. Pigeon's shed sits this Sunday night, as Pigeon curls on his bed, in the late night dull-mute dark of the hill. The shed is almost pitch. There's only the light from the house filtering down, and only the sound of the television in the off-balance house. The television's chatter echoes around the garden, and even into the shed.

In the house Cher and his mam are sitting still still still while He watches the television. It's important not to be noticed. Not to stand out. There should be no sudden noises. No opinions other than His own. There should be nothing but the news on the television, only these tears on the news, a house gone, a family, two children upstairs suffocated by the

21

smoke. There should be nothing else, only Him, drinking a beer, His wife, His daughter, His cigarette, and the house around them.

Cher is sitting very upright, her feet together, as if they're tied. Cher is sitting not watching the television but making sure He's satisfied that she's watching it, just as He's satisfied that she's exactly the kind of girl He wants her to be. Cher's shoes are little pink princess slippers. Her hair's perfectly brushed back into a ponytail, and there's a bow there, which is powder blue. Occasionally, if she catches Him watching her, Cher will make the right expression for the television; a smile if it's funny, a frown for serious, or, for right now, for this family lost in the fire on the news, sadness. Not relief. Perhaps Cher has that letter now? In her pocket. The one the postman gave Pigeon, and he gave to her, so that He couldn't steal it. Pigeon had read it first. It was from someone he'd never met. Martha. That's Cher's sister. Cher said not to mention her name. She lives in Manchester. *Come and live with me, Cher.* Said the letter. *Come to Manchester.* But Cher's too scared of Him even to move in the living room.

In the shed Pigeon's reading, reading with a wind-up torch in the dark. He has to stop every minute or so to wind it. He wears three jumpers, lies in a sleeping bag with a duvet on top his mam's brought down from the house for him.

Pigeon's reading the newspaper, Efa's newspaper he stole. He's reading it line by line. He doesn't understand all the words, but he can read them. He says the words into the shed, and he likes the sounds of the words in the newspaper as they fill the mould that is the shed.

"Exper-i-ment. Acqui-sit-tion. Super-la-tive."

He has a small, cold mouth, and the words fill his mouth too, they fill it with their different textures: clay, metal, soap

22

textures, and the strange tastes of the words as he says them into the cold air.

He turns the page. There are photographs. Pigeon's not interested in the photographs. The words he can taste. He can put the words into his pockets, keep one "extra-ordi-nary" in the space between his gums and his teeth. He can keep one behind his ear, "defen-sive-ly" one he might need at any moment. There's a word in each shoe, a word stuffed down his sleeping bag, the vowels pushing for space like his wriggling legs.

He'll give words to other people too. This is a good way of keeping them. He'll even give words to Cher: like "coll – at – teral" and "expon – ential".

Sometimes, when he and Iola are in the shed, planning, he'll throw a good word out of the shed door as if he doesn't care about it, and watch through the window as Cher grovels on the ground to pick it up, the sounds of it almost slipping through her clumsy lovely sieve fingers. Pigeon likes it when Cher says one of these words, slips it into a sentence about something else. Cher's mouth is warm and soft; the words sound different in her mouth. "Pijin," she says, nervous, "D'you reckon Gwyn's psych-co-logical?"

Pigeon's tried to give his mam some of the words too, when she sits by his side on the bed, when she strokes his hair. He talks, saying the words, "atten-tive", "apa-the-tic", "list-less", or, in Welsh: "di-fa-ter", "di-sby-ddu", "brith-io", trying to give her word after word after word. But she doesn't hear them, she can't hear the words anymore and they fall apart in the air, like snowballs, powdery-white and light. He's learnt not to let too many go on his mam like this. They'll never come back. It's cos of Him. What He's doing to her.

And then Iola. Throwing words her way is like making home-made rockets, shooting them up, watching them explode, crash, or disappear into next door's garden. Half the time they go to waste, the words. She'll be thinking of something else, not listening. But sometimes Iola'll catch a word, wide-eyed. It's like she can't believe she's caught it, by accident, the brightly-coloured ball of a word. Then, she never just holds it, or gives it back, straight, as it is, instead she'll start fiddling with it, throw it in the air a couple of times, stamp on it, press it into a new shape. Half dreaming, she'll pull it in two, make it something different. Sometimes she can make a word a lot worse, like "flourish" becoming "flour ish", sometimes she can make a great word out of two bad ones, like "massakiller", or "sicko-psycho". She'll say the new word slowly, badly, tastily.

But Iola, she doesn't know what to do with a good word she's made. She can't make a good story all by herself, Iola. Or not yet! She'll often just play around with the word, tickle it, play cat and mouse with it until the word almost curls up and.

And he'll snatch it back, brush it off, put it in line, or under the bed with all the others, like a hamster making a nest, or a home.

But he likes her, Iola, as much as he likes anyone. Her games can make a story different, something for Pigeon to use. Iola and Pigeon, this is the way they are.

He turns off the torch and lies in the dark, listening to the muttering television filling the garden, watching the house shadows play around the shed. The house occasionally moves, as if standing in an untenable posture, as if the creases in its muscles have grown sore. The house is silent, there are no words here, only the muttering of the TV, only Cher, Mari, only Him.

Pigeon lies in the dark, and then drifts into an empty, white sleep, curled in the shadow of the house. Dream and nightmare stories about Gwyn and Him babble up around him as night slowly turns its page, until Gwyn and Him are one man, with one pair of hard, painful fists between them.

5

Efa got the idea about chapel last week, in the kitchen, after I told her about Gwyn again.

"Ma Gwyn hufen iâ'n *murderer*," I'd said, the idea of it fizzing on my tongue. "Mae o'n lladd pobl efo'i *bare hands*."

The words tingled and popped in my mouth, but Efa just leant against the worktop in the kitchen looking at me hard, her lips like a zip.

"P'rhaps you should go to chapel on Sundays from now on, Iola," she said then.

"But *you* don't."

"I did go to chapel, back in the day, and everybody should go for a bit."

I crinkled my forehead, huffed through my nose.

"Why are kids supposed to believe in God? Nobody else does."

But Efa wasn't up for a fight. She blanked the 'God!' question.

"Be better for you to be there at Sunday school than eating ice creams and playing stupid games with Pigeon," she said, stirring whatever it was she was pickling on the stove.

The first few chapel Sundays, Efa comes with. Nasareth Chapel's there, on the High Street, weighing the street down. The building scowls as Efa and me walk towards it. The chapel's made of grey stone and it's fat like a lord. It's too big for the small, closed shops, and the square, grey council houses that make up down-town. I can feel 'God!' giving me a headache.

But inside it's bright, and God! isn't around yet, so we're OK. There are lots of ladies who know Efa here. They smell nice and clean, and of scent that's like flowers. They smile at me too. One of them gives me a sweet. That's for coming to Sunday School she says. How old are you love?

I lie. "Deg," I say.

"Iola!" says Efa.

So I have to tell them my real age.

But they aren't angry about me lying, they say it's a white lie. I wonder if 'God!' will agree when he shows up with the minister.

We all file in, and as we walk up the aisle I count how many feet I can see. I lose count at fifty.

"Sh," Efa says. Because I was counting out loud.

We sit and we listen to the minister, and to the singing which fills your whole body up like a balloon so you want to take off up to heaven.

"How come you know all the songs?" I ask Efa.

The lady with the sweet turns round to me and smiles again.

"I like her," I whisper to Efa.

She likes me too, and so I'll be in her Sunday school class after the service says Efa.

There are three other girls in her class. Damn. I know them from school. I don't like them and they don't like me. At school last week Catrin had told the class that I stink. It's because of all Efa's incense. I keep telling Efa not to burn it, but she says it's good for her soul. What about mine? A soul is the bit of grown ups that can get sick and keep them awake at night. Chapel is where you grow one. I'm not sure I want that.

But the teacher is really nice. And she tells Catrin off for not smiling and giving me a welcome when I join the class. Catrin just scowls. I can see the teacher, who's called Anti Siwan, watching Catrin. She watches her, and you can tell that if it wasn't for God! she'd have got angry. So I like her even more. Only Efa or Pigeon usually stick up for me.

All the ladies at chapel are called Anti. Although they aren't really, worse luck. Mind you, I wouldn't want Anti Gladys even if she was mine.

"Wel bore da, Efa Williams!" says Anti Gladys, as soon as we walk in through the heavy door of the chapel the second Sunday. "Ers talwm iawn," *long time no see*, she says, licking her pink lipstick, sour-puss mouth. "We were here last week!" says Efa. But Anti Gladys can't have noticed us last week, cos she looks like she doesn't believe that.

Anti Gladys wears a posh coat and, although she's old and creased, still has long boobs and green all round her eyes. Siwan's behind her, and I see her frown, and meet Efa's eye.

"Bore da, Gladys," Efa says it quiet, stood there in the musty vestry in her long, glitter skirt and her gypsy headscarf, looking like she's there by mistake. I'm stood next to her, itchy in my woolly tights, my blue raincoat, and my red velvet Sunday dress. The dress is too small now, pinches under the arms. I need the loo, stand on my right foot with my left foot.

The air in the chapel's full of the smells of clean people

again. Across the vestry I can hear them whispering. The girls. Rhiannon and Catrin. They giggle at me and shoot glares that mean watch out. I give them a heavy look, and, while Anti Gladys and Efa pretend to have a conversation, I stick out my blue, gobstopper-stained tongue. The girls gasp all dramatic at me so Anti turns and catches me in the act. "Un o'r teulu?" she asks Efa, syrup sweet. One of the family is she?

I look up at Anti Gladys. She smiles. But it's not like Anti Siwan. It's like the cover of a magazine. Not real.

"What are you dressed up for, dear?" Anti asks Efa in her snobby Welsh. "A Christmas pantomime?"

Efa stays away after that week, and Anti Gladys' sharp tongue. Now she just takes me up to the steps in front of the serious building, looks up at the chapel doors like she dreads it, and backs off before Anti Siwan or any of the other Antis catch her and hoik her in. Anti Siwan goes out after her the first week, but even she can't persuade Efa to come in again. For all her hippy clothes and colours, Efa's like a closed door. She looks upset, but she just won't budge.

I have to walk the steps to the wooden doors myself. Anti Siwan stretches her hand out for mine, but I don't take it, I don't want the girls to think I'm a baby. I walk into the chapel on my own, find a seat at the back where I can open my comic and read while the sermon and the songs fall blunt and hollow into the gallery. The songs are my favourite bit of chapel so far. I sit and listen to the hymns as they swell up like a kite and then go all the way to heaven through the sagging chapel roof.

After the service it's Sunday school, and I look out of the classroom window at the mountains which are snowy like vienetta, I think about Pigeon and while Anti Siwan talks about 'Iesu!' those shaky ice-cream tunes play in my head. I try for a while, to think about 'Jesus!' and his beard and his fish and his bread, but then I think about Gwyn's Ice Creams instead. I line up the ice creams to choose my favourite. Which is chocolate. Always chocolate.

"Iola Williams stinks," says Catrin, in her wasp's voice. Siwan's gone out the room. Sitting next to Catrin, Rhiannon giggles in her matching dress, her matching spite.

"Iola Williams stinks like silage. Iola Williams' dress is too small for her. Iola Williams' mam isn't her real mam. Iola Williams' mam's dead. Have you seen her sister? She's a proper freak."

Chocolate was definitely the best, I can taste it. Anyway, thing is about Efa, she takes all these pills to keep her soul healthy, and everyone laughs at her because of the beads and the colours, but really she's more alive than any of them, any of them who talk about her behind their snatchy dead hands and roll their eyes like marbles under their grey hair when she passes.

I ask Efa about them when I get home.

"Why aren't they all nice with you, Efa?"

"Lots of them are lovely."

"Yes but…"

"Anti Gladys is just old and old fashioned," says Efa.

I wait. Efa will tell me if I wait.

"She was one of the ones who told tales about our family, back in the day. She told all the old people here that Nain was a tart."

"Why?"

"Because Dad had no Dad and Nain hadn't got married."

"So?"

"So it used to matter."

"Getting married?"

"Getting married before you had kids."

"But it doesn't anymore?"

"Not so much."

"Not to Anti Siwan?"

Efa laughs. "Anti Siwan doesn't give a toss either way," she says "*She's* nice."

I smile. Anti Siwan is lovely.

I like it at chapel. I like the being part of it. And how my voice with all of theirs singing makes one big proud voice, and from what they tell me about him, I even like Jesus. Sharing and all that. And all the little things being important. Like me.

But even Jesus and the singing, and Anti Siwan and the other ones who smell of flowers and smile, and even the being a part of it, this huge thing, even that doesn't cancel out missing Pigeon. Compared to chapel, compared to anything, Sundays with Pigeon are one big ride. He's making it up as he goes along and you just want to make sure you're in on it. Well in. Compared to that, chapel is all polish smells, pretty, uncomfortable dresses, girls pinching, and boys getting the credit for everything.

"Why do I have to go if you don't?" I ask her.

Efa looks at me.

"You need to learn how to live in society," she says like a robot.

"You mean be good?"

"Yes."

"Like you?" I don't mean it like a joke but she laughs. She gives me a hug, but she still makes me go.

What Efa didn't reckon on, what no one reckoned on ever, was on Pigeon, and Pigeon deciding to come to Sunday school too, after being bored without me for a couple of pretend-schoolday-Sundays and not being able to go home in case of his mam.

Anti Gladys looks at Pigeon's grey school trousers in *that* way. She turns her nose when she sees me and Pigeon, and steps away from us, like a spider steps sideways when you poke its web. Anti Gladys only smiles at Mr Lewis the minister, standing beside God! up on the pulpit.

Rhiannon and Catrin stay away from us too. That's good. Sitting on a pew all of our own, Pigeon and me pretend to whisper to each other about the girls. Pigeon'll just make noises, or sing things in my ear. The laugh'll come right up from my belly and out my nose then. And some of the people will turn round and look cross. Even though Siwan smiles when she turns, she puts her finger on her lips to say be quiet. But Pigeon doesn't listen.

Sometimes Pigeon says whole jokes in my ear, when he can think of them.

"Catrin has a fanny made of slugs," Pigeon says into my ear one time. I don't like him saying it. Fanny. I don't like Pigeon saying that word.

Pigeon tells me how much more fun we're having at chapel now than I was having when I came on my own. It must be true. It's much better after Pigeon starts coming, and his ideas drawing moustaches and willies on Jesus and the disciples in the picture-bible in the vestry. He draws the willies in, long and dangly, with thick black felt-tip. Even Mr Lewis looks like he wants to laugh then cause, reading something about "God!" and stuff at me and Pigeon, he's shaking all over, looking down and pointing a wobble finger at us while we're stood in front of the pulpit with everyone else watching from all the benches that go back and back with the nice young Antis and the old Antis on them, until they reach the door of the chapel where I want to be running out.

But when I turn round I can see that Anti Siwan and some of the other young women are crying because they're trying so hard not to laugh. I think it's because of them that Mr Lewis decides we should take a week off Sunday school, and just go home and tell Efa what we've done, fat chance. Anti Gladys offers to walk us out of chapel. She's loving it.

She walks us out onto the empty street, and then looks down at us with her painted face. Then she says it. She leans down, so her face is at the level of Pigeon's and she says, very quietly, so that none of the others can hear: "F off".

Pigeon and me run off down the street. Pigeon's laughing and whooping, and I'm copying him, although I'm a bit shocked.

"We made Anti Gladys say 'fuck'," says Pigeon. "Well, almost." And we're pretty pleased.

But as we're running away I can hear all the singing coming from inside the big bear chapel, and a bit of me wishes I was in there with Siwan and Jesus and the flower scents, and even with the pretty mean girls in their Sunday dresses, and the old people sagging and singing all together like wolves. I was part of it, and now we're out, and it's just Pigeon and me.

6

He needed her. Without Iola, all his thoughts just made a black inky mess. It was telling her that put it all in order. So when he went round to hers, and Efa was there on her own, saying Iola was out at chapel, he thought why not?

He scuffed his feet up the road, pulled open the heavy door, and just walked in, right in the middle of the sermon. Everyone turned round as he walked down the aisle, looking for Iola.

She grabbed him from behind and dragged him after her to the back row. He sat down. Some of the people looked at each other, raising eyebrows, but he just sat down, and it was like he could just stay. Maybe he could?

But it was too much, really to try to put yourself in the middle of it, the town. To go to chapel, and have your voice rise with the others in the long, swelling songs that made you ache from the inside out. It was too much, when all you'd ever done was stand outside of it. And especially when that woman, the teacher, treated you as if you belonged. It was too much. Pigeon could feel that he wanted to tell her. About Him. He could feel that she was the kind of person that might care. The words were dangerous, crowding to the tip of his tongue. If you said them, they might smash it all up, the pictures and stories you had to have to hold your own world together. The words that were almost on Pigeon's tongue, almost working their way out, to be whispered in Siwan's ear, almost, those words had the power to undo it all. And Pigeon couldn't. He couldn't say them.

So he'd just smash all this up instead: Iola's Sundays without him, the chapel. Those people who cared and the others who didn't. He'd smash it into so many bits with his words, that Iola wouldn't want any of it any more. She'd just want him. And he didn't care about God! either. God! was just another version of Him. Watching everyone all the time, and making them do and behave the way He wanted, threatening them, and throwing some of them out to live in the shed. Pigeon hated Him. So he wasn't about to listen to God's songs and their strange achey chorus. He wasn't about to let Iola enjoy any of it. He'd have to drag her away. He'd have to cut the cord that linked her, by the belly button, to the town.

The best way was to mess up their story. And their story was the bible. So he'd get in there with his felt tip, and he'd turn it all inside out. Pigeon could undo any story he wanted. He'd done that all his life. Breaking up words and gluing them back together. Mr Lewis felt it. Pigeon knew he did. Mr Lewis knew exactly what Pigeon was trying to do. That was why he was so angry. He knew it wasn't about being funny. It wasn't just willies and boobs on the bible, like the ladies who were laughing thought. This was a fight. And it was deadly serious.

Pigeon wanted her back. Everyone needs someone to listen to them when they tell their story. Everyone needs that. Iola was essential. She was, like it said in Efa's newspaper 'utterly ir-re-place-a-ble'. He needed to get them to show they didn't care about her as much as he did.

35

"F off," said that woman. And so he'd won.

He'd got her back. He'd pushed all of that ache away. He'd not told a soul. And now they could get on with it, him and Iola. The Gwyn story. They could tell it along together.

7

Sitting in Pigeon's attic is way, way better than chapel anyway, and now Pigeon's smoking "which," like he says, "you can't do in Sunday school and that's why it's crap."

In Pigeon's house He's out, and taken Pigeon's mam off somewhere on the bus, and Cher too, but not Pigeon, so Pigeon and me can sit in the triangle attic, hiding from Efa, and He's not here to care. For once there's no Cher even, being a pain and asking difficult questions. From the attic window I can see the houses piling up and up the hill, and just hear the tapered ends of all the noises in the valley – the quarry bangs, the cars growling like dogs, the beep and grind of quarry trucks loading and reversing, loading and reversing across the layered slate tips, even on a Sunday. Up here where Pigeon's house pushes into the sky, with windows turned to the clouds, Pigeon and me are making our plan.

He's bending his long arms and legs round the chair and table like wet willow for bows and arrows, one of His cigarettes behind one ear and his thumb grinding at the sparky wheel of a lighter, His, like the cigarette and the twenty pound note Pigeon shows me, stuffed down his pants between his white skinny belly and the elastic.

"Twenty quid, Iola!" he says, showing it off, and grinning. Pigeon's smile's like the wood stove in my and Efa's cold kitchen, too small to heat the whole room, but still better than nothing, that's Pigeon's smile.

It stinks, but Pigeon loves to smoke. So now he's pinching the cigarette from behind his right ear and holding it between finger and thumb, lifting the white tube of the thing to his mouth, then sucking on it so his mouth looks small round the cigarette. While he sucks he's flicking the wheel of the lighter all at the same time to light it. Pigeon looks smaller when he smokes. The cigarette makes him look like a real little boy, like when I put on Efa's make-up. Smoke comes out his mouth: disgusting, pretty, sweet and bitter, and this is way better than Sunday school anyway.

With the windows open for the smoke to get away, we're bending over the map, which Pigeon says is "of here, the hill, and the town, and the river, and there, the mountains too". On the map, when Pigeon wrestles it round to look, is a little red cross "where Gwyn's house is".

I'm in on it this time, well in, and on the way to that little red cross, red like blood on the map. I'm Pigeon's right hand man in her itchy tights and Sunday dress.

"We go there," says Pigeon, in English like in the films, "and we give him a … a…"

"…taste of his own medication?" I finish it.

"Ia," says Pigeon. "Ia. That's right."

We're filling our pockets with weapons: a penknife for me, a lighter for Pigeon, stones with sharp teeth, "ready to take out an eye", Pigeon says. He brings a length of rope and a hankerchief too, "for a gag". He looks up at me as he says it. His eyes are like deep water. Pigeon stands by the attic window. He's dark against the white day outside. Then I see how his hands are shaking a bit. He's cross. No, not cross. Angry. Why is he so angry?

But I just have to do what Pigeon says. I have to believe what he says and do it all. That's Pigeon.

In our pockets we put drawing pins, a pen, the map, the twenty-pound note, a reel of cellotape, a torch, batteries, a catapult, and a banana.

"It's Dewi's birthday," I tell Efa. Dewi's a boy from Pigeon's class who lost a tooth last week and spent the money on stinkbombs for Pigeon's coat so Pigeon "wouldn't be seen dead going to his party" but it makes a good story to tell Efa. Efa's all happy chanting a Yoga song in the backroom when we call over to tell her about the party. She shoos us away and we race down the hill to catch the number 67 out of here.

By the time we're getting onto the bus, I'm already feeling something strange, something ice and still sitting around my ribs. But it's enough to worry about just being on a bus that's different and going to somewhere else, down the hill and off onto the main road on the bus with all the old people and the bus driver, who just raises his eyebrows at Pigeon's twenty pound note, looks down at me and sighs "hh", shaking his head like that, while we go along between the seats, right to the back.

With the map open across us, Pigeon's counting down the streets of the town while we're leaving it: "Stryd Goronwy, Stryd Albert, Stryd Uchaf, Stryd Ganol, Stryd Isaf, Stryd Syth, Stryd Gam, Stryd y Gwynt, Stryd y Glaw," and out onto the main road like spit from a pea shooter.

"D'you see?"

While the bus rattles like a money box, Pigeon's pointing to where we are on the map with his finger. The finger's moving along the road, closer to the red cross – closer and closer and closer, so I stop looking, cos I feel sick. I'm sick cos of the bus, but also because I want to rub out the red biro of the cross and move Pigeon's finger back along the lines on the map until it comes to 'Rallt Uchaf' and my house again at the top of the hill, with Efa probably doing the Shifassanna sleepy thing after her Yoga by now. And I feel that sick feeling again because it's not Gwyn I'm scared of anymore, it's Pigeon, and I'd give anything to curl up next to Efa and breathe in and out through her nose while Efa listens to the stupid guy on the tape, saying in, out, in, out, in, out, in.

When Pigeon and me get off the bus, we're on a flat street, where all the houses are separate, and white, and they all have small gardens and it's nice. It's very quiet though, so quiet because there's not so much weather down here. The sky's high above us, and there's no one on the street at all.

"How'd you know he'll be in anyways?" I ask Pigeon.

"Cos I asked him how long his shifts were, stupid, and he said he gets home at four every day."

Pigeon has the map, and he also has this piece of paper, with an address on it. The number he's looking for is seventeen. The house we're closest to says seventy-seven, so we're a long way off and have to walk all the way down the street, all the way down on the black pavement. The things I have in my pockets are making a din. I go down the street making such a noise that Pigeon says "Iolaaaaaa" like that, like as if it's my fault.

"Can't help it can I!" I say back, because it's true. I can't do anything to stop any of this. That's the thing. That's the truth.

"Hold those pockets then," he says, and I can tell he's nervous too now so I do what he says, holding my pockets with my hands, and we walk down the quiet, empty road like that. I only make a noise sometimes.

Number seventeen is one quarter of one of the big houses; a big house split up like a chocolate bar into little flats. Number seventeen is one of the flats. Pigeon looks at it, looks at the small shoebox that's number seventeen, and he looks like a balloon that's lost its air. Gwyn's always rich in Pigeon's stories. Pigeon's even angrier now things don't fit in. That's not good for me. That's not good for Gwyn.

Pigeon says "Stay here, Iola."

And I do. I wait, standing just outside Gwyn's garden. Except Gwyn doesn't have a garden. He has gravel and one rose in the middle with some rocks that are the same colour as gravel in a little circle round the dead rose.

Pigeon goes up to the window of number seventeen. He goes so close that I feel hot and sick. My shoulders and my chest are burning all of a sudden with all the fear of Pigeon going up to the window. Pigeon's looking into the room now. He looks for a few seconds, then he comes back to me.

"He's there," he says.

"O," I say.

"He's planning," says Pigeon in Welsh, and then changes to English like in the films "*Planning his next terrible crime*," says Pigeon.

I shiver. And I want to see too, want to see Gwyn in there planning what he's going to do next, and to who, and it's like when you think you can fly, and you forget what's real and what's not, and forget you're not brave enough, and it's like that, when all of a sudden, I'm at the window, like Pigeon was before.

Inside, it's quite dark, and looks like old cupboards smell. It's a living room, but it looks dead. Like a kind of a coffin. Everything's a pale brown. There's a sofa and two armchairs all in the same colour. Apart from that, there's a glass topped coffee table and some plastic flowers in a pot in the middle of the table. And there's Gwyn, on the sofa. The murderer. I can see his hairy neck, and the shiny round top of his head, and I can see his stubby hands and they're...

He's just doing a crossword.

Which I don't say anything about to Pigeon. Pigeon looks annoyed enough already, cos it's not going like in his stories, not really. Gwyn just looks boring, and his house is boring too, but I don't say it.

"Be nawn ni ta?" I whisper the question to Pigeon when we're both back on the street side of Gwyn's garden wall, away from the house enough to talk. He doesn't answer, doesn't know what to do next, that's what I reckon. Perhaps he's making this up as he goes along. Perhaps he'll give up now that it's not really working. Except I'm not sure I want that to be a crossword, and Gwyn to be an ice-cream man, and this to be a quiet boring street with no fast weather and no other story either.

"Awn ni mewn?"

Pigeon doesn't usually ask questions. Which is good, cos I don't much like choosing answers. Like now, I really don't know. But I nod.

Pigeon looks surprised. I'm surprised too, because that was a crazy thing to do: nod. Then Pigeon nods too, and he starts walking toward the house again, like as if he was the one that was brave and decided to go in, not me.

I stand out by the rose, try telling myself I'm here in case Gwyn gets up and starts moving, so I can warn Pigeon, but it's a lie, really I'm just here cos I can't move a toe or a finger with all the burning chills I have in my bones and all over. Then I see Gwyn standing up.

I still can't move. But Gwyn doesn't see me stood by his dead rose in the grey garden. He walks away from the window, and goes through a door to the back, which isn't good: that's where Pigeon is too. And I can't move, still can't move.

Next minute Pigeon comes running out, his coat over his head to hide his face. Pigeon runs. Pigeon runs towards me. "Run, Iola! Run!" he shouts at me, his face white as he grabs my arm and we both run off down the road. And although I can't hear anything coming behind and I don't look until Gwyn's gone, Gwyn must be running down the street after us with a knife, cos Pigeon says.

We get to the bus stop and hide inside. Pigeon stands looking out of it down the road. Ydi Gwyn yn dwad, Pigeon? Is he coming? Pigeon, is Gwyn coming? Is Gwyn coming after us, Pigeon?

"No. Stupid. Don't be an idiot, " he says. And that's when I know why Pigeon's cross. Pigeon's cross and so he says I'm stupid, and it's cos we haven't been able to use the stones and the rope and the hankerchief gag, or any of the other things. We're too scared of Gwyn and his crossword and his boring house.

I don't say anything on the bus, just hold my pockets trying to stop the stuff in them clunking when the bus shakes round the corners and uphill to our town and the blown-up clouds again. I don't say anything. Pigeon doesn't say anything either.

I give him another chance when we're off the bus. "What happened? What happened, Pigeon?" I ask him.

Maybe he'll say he saw all Gwyn's knives there, round the back, or he saw lots of babies' graves or he saw somebody all tied up and kidnapped and saw Gwyn sharpening his knives when he left the crossword in the living room, or that Gwyn saw him and threatened to kill him, that'd be good.

But Pigeon doesn't say anything. So Pigeon just saw Gwyn and he got a big fright, cos he's a prissy hogan after all. But I don't say that. Pigeon's my best friend.

Cher's come to meet us on the road, asking in English, "Did you get him did you get him, Pigeon did you get him?" And Pigeon just mutters, "I will", with a murderer's voice and pushes past Cher like he's storming through a door. And then there's just me, because I don't believe Pigeon, not really, and he knows it. And there's just me, there on the street on my own, and Pigeon's angry with me. And when he's angry with me, he just walks away. But I don't care. I don't care. I don't follow him. I turn round to walk home to Efa not caring at all. And when I look after him again he's stomping along the street towards his house and the shed, with Cher running behind, asking him "How, Pigeon, how?" because Cher's stupid really and will believe anything.

8

Pigeon's furious, a cold, frightened fury, as he walks along home. And as Cher trails beside him down the meandering, skinny road, saying, "Be careful Pigeon, someone from school came and told them you weren't there. Dad's angry, He's really angry." Pigeon, going home to another beating sure enough, hates Gwyn, hates him with a kind of cumulative, pressurised anger.

The anger had started, originially, because of what had happened between Gwyn and Him.

Things in the house had been getting worse and worse. There was no work in the town, or nothing for a dockworker, used to industrial shipping, timetabling and operating big cranes that were as big as monsters. There was nothing here on the hill. There were money problems.

Finally He got a job as a bouncer in the new club in the next town. It was good, because He was out at night, bad, because it was paid badly and because it made Him dark round the eyes and angry, and taught Him to use His heavy, hard hands.

"Mari," He said last month, "I don't know how we'll get to the end of the month, darling."

And then it was, "You'll have to work faster, Mari. Work faster."

They only had her dresses, and the letters she'd address and post for that company. You had to do hundreds a day to make any money on that. There were weeks where they couldn't pay the rent. They ate absolutely everything from tins, because it was cheaper. They couldn't afford the electric heater in Pigeon's shed anymore. They couldn't afford warmth for Pigeon, but He still sat drinking beers in the living room all day.

Cher was afraid of Him. You could see in her eyes, and her hands. She almost jumped when He spoke.

Pigeon couldn't bear it. There was something wrong in the way He made Cher wear pretty dresses all the time, and be perfect. Pigeon couldn't bear to be around her. She was everything He wanted her to be. Cher was his "darling girl". That's what He said. And He was sick.

He hated Pigeon. He hated him. It was all Pigeon's fault. Pigeon got it all, all the anger about not having enough money, all the anger about the bad job, about not being able to stop with the beer, about not being able to stop keeping Cher all boxed up and perfect like a doll, and about what was happening to Mari, since He had started locking away her words and expressions one by one, until she had nothing left to say.

Once she could barely speak up for herself anymore, He stopped her moving. Stilled her. Made her stay at home. Locked her in even. Wouldn't let her go out alone. So that her street, her town were no longer hers, and even her boy, Pigeon, was shut away from her, wasn't hers.

But that particular Sunday, because of the beating Pigeon'd got for stealing that lolly, and because last week Efa'd given him the money, she said.

"I hate it that they bought you one out of pity for us." She looked almost angry. She's funny his mum. She's not brave, but she does have this thing. This thing in her. *Pride*, Efa'd called it. *Pride*.

"Look Pigeon," showing him her purse. "I can get one for the both of you."

It was odd, seeing her out on the street again. How she seemed to grow with every step, until you think maybe, maybe He won't fit her back in through the door again, because she'll be too proud and tall and beautiful. Maybe she'll escape.

"What'll you have?" she asked him as they walked along the street towards the van and she was half smiling, "a Feast? Or a Calypso?"

He considered. "I'll wait and see what she chooses," he said after a while. "It's her turn."

He liked the idea of buying Iola an ice cream. Being big about it. Offering her a choice. It'd taste different, better, knowing it was his own mam that bought it. And, when Pigeon saw Gwyn, for a moment he was just an ice-cream man, nothing to worry about, a guy.

Pigeon's mam went up to the slot in the van's side.

"One Feast. One Calypso."

And Gwyn changed. He changed like men do with her. He looked down at her, and he smiled and he said what a nice day it was, and what did a pretty young thing like her want today, and Pigeon's mam, you couldn't believe it, Pigeon's mam laughed and she said "well, I'm after two ice creams." And she told him which and he got one out and he winked at her as he handed it over, and she laughed again. And the thing wouldn't have been so bad, except she was seen.

He was coming up the road with Cher, and He saw her there, saw the wink. He had her arm straight away, and pulled her away from the van walking her up the street towards the house. Pigeon

47

left the van, and Gwyn, staring and ran with them. He ran after them right to the door to the house, his breath tight in his chest. Pigeon got there just behind them, but He dragged her inside anyway, and slammed the door in Pigeon's face. And you couldn't get in. You couldn't get in, and Pigeon kicked and kicked, he kicked and kicked the door, and she cried, she cried inside.

The police came that day. It was because Pigon ran to Iola's. Efa called them. They came, and that stopped Him. But then they went again. His mam sent them away.

She had bruises. "It's ok, love," she said, when Pigeon cried over her bruises. "Bruises fade."

But it wasn't true. That wasn't true for Pigeon.

Though she did wince, did cower, did cry quiet bewildered tears, she didn't carry Adrian's anger, not like Pigeon did. It was Pigeon that took all His anger about the mess it all was, and how it wouldn't sit tidy, not even for Him, the anger about what He was doing to His 'love', to Mari as He fought with her to keep her in control. Pigeon got it all. Pigeon took it all, and he took the second beating, the beating that was to spare, when He came to the shed, shaking with the rage of it, and with not being able to stop.

And now, again, Adrian is at the door, shouting.

"Open the damned door!" he shouts. "Open it right now or I'll fuckin' kill you. I will."

Today will be like the other days. Threats. Bruises. Threats.

Pigeon sits on his bed, his knees drawn up to his chest. He sits, watching a tiny ant crawl over the doorframe, watching his shed become a whole wide world to the ant. Pigeon sits, and he waits for the beating, and he hates, he hates Gwyn with all his might.

9

Efa will be home, with her million and one herbs and yoga and meditation and pills and grains and breathing exercises. A million and one things which can't make up for the fact that Efa's not really happy, and her life's no fun. When I open the door, sure enough, there's Efa, listening to music, and she's in one of her moods, her good moods. Too good.

Efa collects songs. She collects them in her head and on paper and on the black records that scratch away ghostly lovely in the cottage where we live. Some of the records are Dad's. The others come through the post. They're the only treat Efa gets with her wages. I've not heard this record before.

"This song," says Efa without even saying hello, "this is a tinker tune."

The man on the record has a voice like brillo. You can't understand him, although he's speaking in English. I slump down at the kitchen table, prop my elbows up and put my chin in my hands to listen. My head's heavy after the Gwyn thing and Pigeon. When the man's finished his song there's a long clickety silence before the next one.

It's a slow deep song with a fiddle and a woman singing.

"Sad isn't it? So sad," says Efa all quiet in her slate Welsh "It's in a language called Yiddish."

It's like losing Dad.

We listen to a few more verses of the song in the dark kitchen, and then Efa gets up, switches it off.

"Lets change it," she says, with thin lips.

"I know," she says, looking through the records on the shelf, "how bout the one with that woman singing in Norwegian?"

Norwegian is when you sing through your nose the same way Mrs Thomas at school speaks posh English for show. When I listen to the song I can see the Norwegian lady all the way over there across the grey sea sitting on a wood stool and singing through her nose. I watch the ink disk of the record turning round and round for the Norwegian lady's voice.

After that The Cuban Song spins on the record player. Efa's favourite record. It's slinky like treacle. "Secsi!" Efa says about it, laughing, and shaking her beads as she dances round the kitchen, while, on a dusty stage someplace and sometime else shaking bottoms dance behind the twanging guitar strings of The Cuban Song. I copy my sister, dancing, and clucking with giggles. It's as if Pigeon and the Gwyn thing never happened. It's as if everything's just fine.

Efa's like this. Sometimes she's so happy she's going to burst. She has to dance and sing, and run around, and if anyone tries to stop her she'll explode like a bottle of Lucozade that's fizzed over. Then she breaks and it's bad. She cries, and there's no end to it. She cries and she cries, and it hurts to see and hear.

It's because of me. It's because Efa has to work all these hours at The Home just to keep me in clothes and hot water. Since Nain died, there's been only me and Efa. And even now, although I'm dancing and laughing, you can't forget it. Cos there's something hurt about Efa, although she's full of swaying skirts and music from all over. There's something hard inside, something that's like Nain.

Nain'd moved in back when Mam was sick. Nain moved in cos of Dad and his long fingers that did nothing except make shapes in the clay, the metal, the wood of the strange, rotting people that still stand, wrapped with bindweed in the garden. Nain came because of the flood in the bathroom Dad made when he fixed the shower, and the explosion in the kitchen when he tried out the pressure cooker, and the way he dyed all our knickers blue with his new overalls. Nain came cos he couldn't look after Mam. He couldn't cope, Dad. He could never cope.

Mam was sick forever. It was the tumours in her head. There was a picture of tumours in Efa's big Family Health book. They're like dark flowers, blooming, and putting the person out. And that was what happened to her. Mam. That was the way it went. And it wasn't because of me. But then why is Efa angry sometimes, so she looks at me like that?

After Mam went to bed sick. It was Efa, me, Dad.

And Nain. It was Nain.

Nain moved in with rules, dinner on the table, and bedtime like a stone wall. Nain with her stories of the town 'back in the day', her slate quarry stories, about when there were no machines and just men, no trucks and drills, about singing and drinking and Sunday times, about Friday paydays and Saturday fights, about rough, dangerous work in the quarries, people dying young and filling up the slate graveyard. Nain was all about wars and dying boys, and women at home, "women's troubles, women's pains". She was all about "back in the day", Nain.

"It's a world unfair for women, love," she'd say, and her voice cracked like worn paint. It's a world unfair for women, love. A world unfair. For women. Love.

"Those men," said Nain looking with pointing eyes at Dad, "you've got to watch them. They only up and leave."

It was because of Taid, or grandfather. It was cos he "went and died in Spain". Nain only ever said it once, but it stuck. Spain was all big frilly dresses and maracas and beating your feet on the floor. Spain was the Olympics in Barcelona. All hot, blue skies and burning colours, and breaking records. When you said it, that Taid "went and died in Spain", it was like a curry in your mouth: too hot, but good and you didn't know what was in it. I said it to Pigeon once.

"Taid went and died in Spain," I said.

Pigeon looked at me. "What does that mean?" he asked me.

I shrugged. "I dunno," I said. "He went there, and he died," I said, after thinking about it for a while.

"I'll go and die in the United States of America," said Pigeon. "Like Elvis Presley and JFK."

"Yeah," I said, although I didn't know what JFK stood for. "Yeah me too," I said again, cos that was the way it was with me and Pigeon.

Nain had it so clear.

"It's a Dad's job to work," she said. "Get back to work, Gerwyn," she said over and over to her son, our dad. I can remember her saying it, and the arguments. "Get yourself a job," she'd say. "Stuff the sculptures, the ornaments, the furniture. Bread and good butter are what homes are made of, Gerwyn. Bread and good butter." And Nain was only going to play Mam, if he'd play Dad.

And playing Dad was being hardly ever there. He'd got

work at the food factory. He put chicken in packets. He worked a particular set of machines which vacuum packed it, stretching the plastic over the slippy chicken. The meat couldn't breathe under the plastic. You could see it. It couldn't breathe. Dad brought some of it home. I can remember it, the meat, all squashed and dead.

There was only the mortuary, where they put Mam in her best dress and in a coffin, and then it was the funeral. In the funeral I stood between everybody's legs while they sang, and while they read things from the old-fashioned Welsh of The Bible. Then it was the heather ground of the hill's graveyard. And in the coffin there was Mam, and even though she was as thin as a baby tree, she was heavy. You could see Dad and the men were struggling with the weight of her, and at the end they almost dropped her into the cold hill. Then everyone prayed to 'god!' and you were supposed to go home.

Nain said it was "the only way".

"Wipe your hands and back to work or whisky," she said to Dad, patting him on the back like a dog.

But he hung about with a lost look by the side of the grave, just all the dull gorse bushes and the dead bracken on the hill behind him. Efa tried to go to him, but Nain pulled her arm.

"He's just maudling," Nain said "Leave him to it. It does no good to share grief, love."

Grief was when you had the heavy thing round your ribs and you couldn't even cry.

He couldn't take it. Not Dad. Efa says he couldn't take it. Efa says Nain had this idea. About men. You had to be like a bull. Strong. You had to earn money and be a "real man" and Dad couldn't do it, Efa says.

He went on years: years of working at the factory. And, at

home, there was just Nain. Nain, in the kitchen, making smooth, empty jam.

Back then Nain was the only one who sang. Sang perfect, stiff folk songs, the ones you learnt at school for Eisteddfod competitons. Nain sang them too pretty and too neat, this tidy kind of happiness in the way she sang them.

"Molianwn oll yn llo – o – on!" she'd sing, or "Tw rym di ro!" or "Migldi Magldi hei now now! Ffaldiradilidalym!"

Nain's tidy folksongs were a lie, like those pretty tea-towels they sell in Pringles to the blue-rinsed tourists, the ones that say 'Wales' all vague at the top. When Nain sang you could tell she wanted to break the grey quiet of the house and Dad's old record-player which sat under dust. She wanted to rub out his hymns and his music from all over, did Nain.

He spoke less and less. He couldn't get them out, his words. Then his breath disappeared like his words. He hung from his bones like empty clothes, and his skin was pale as if it couldn't breathe, like the meat he put in packets at the food factory. Then he started to talk again, but not to anyone, just to himself.

"Air," he said. "I need air. Air," over and over.

It was spring and there were birds singing the day he went.

When I came home from school that day, there was Nain, sat at the table, a cold cup of tea undrunk in her hands, and her eyes staring straight ahead. There was Efa stood perfectly still in the middle of the kitchen. Efa's face was white as milk and round the three of us the house was empty. When Nain spoke she just said, "He's left us, love. He's left us."

We looked for him all over. There was nothing left. Only the quiet house and, down at the bottom of the garden, a shape made of wood which had swelled up with the rain. It was a man, the shape. I go to look at it sometimes now, and it's a man, stooping.

And after that you couldn't speak about him. Like his father. He was just like his father.

"Way it'll always be. All they do is leave you, men, all they ever do, leave you to it." Nain said. "Like *him*. Off to Spain. As if it mattered! As if it mattered to people here what happened there. As if it mattered, for god's sake!"

She meant Taid, our grandpa. She couldn't speak about Dad without getting him mixed up with Taid.

Nain stayed. And Dad's junk was cleared out from the corners, hard daylight was let right into the smoky dust of the house. Nain filled the kitchen with the smells of home, but Efa and me kept looking. It was a game of hide and seek and we were searching for something, something that wasn't quite certain. We were looking for creaking floorboards, walls that moved a bit. We were looking for Dad.

Nain watched us. "It's this place that's the trouble. This hill. Cursed place it is. Rotten," and, when we kept dragging our feet all round the house, "Nothing good comes of people here," she said "There's no dreams, that's the trouble, only closed shops. There's far too much doubt here. That's the trouble."

Nain started entering prize draws. Efa and her made up English poems for magazine competitions, sent in jokes, riddles, whatever it took. One time we won seventy-five quid for one, and it was printed, under a pretend name: "Mrs Thatcher from Leicester," Nain had put. "Address not supplied."

"Why not, 'Mrs Evans from Rallt Uchaf', Nain?" I couldn't see why not.

"Chei di'm lwc yn fanma 'sdi, nghariad i." *You'll get nowhere from here, love. You'll get nowhere. Here is nowhere.*

So Efa and me are going to The Ends of the Earth. We're

going to a place called Jamaica. We're going to Australia and Uzbekistan. Efa has lots of ideas. But now she just works in The Home.

We'd run out of money. It was Nain who'd got Efa the job at The Home. She'd got Efa to leave school for that job. It didn't make sense. Nain doesn't make sense. Now it's all old people and changing them and cleaning them and talking to them all day. That's all it is for Efa now. There are no escape plans anymore.

Even before Nain died, Efa'd started playing Mam. At night I crawled into her bed, and we whispered stories. First it is Efa, Efa that tells the stories. They are about places like Thailand and Belize where people don't have knives and forks. They are about China and Japan where everyone slept on the floor and so their backs were straight like pencils.

I'd come home and found Nain lying on the floor. And you knew she was dead because she didn't move. She was still and yellow and unhappy lying on the floor. And the light was still off, she'd not turned it on since the daytime although it was dark now, so you knew.

We did the funeral thing again. There weren't many people there in chapel for the funeral. Nain was older than Mam. Older people have less friends. It's better to die when you're not too old.

"She never married," said the minister standing in the pulpit above our nain in her square box, "but had one son."

Why did the old ladies look at each other like that? Efa's hand gripped mine. Why did the minister make Efa angry?

It was after that Efa'd got out Dad's record player, and started with the music and the bright colours and all. Because you could.

With Nain gone, you could do anything, except leave The Home.

Efa'd run out, run out of ideas by the time bedtime came, she was so busy with The Home, with the house, with money and getting by. So I started collecting stories.

"He just went," Efa'd always told me, "upped and left. Just like that." And then, "It's a world unfair for women, love." Efa said, saying it just like Nain. But I looked at her and thought how the two of them, Nain dressed in a dull pinny and slippers, and Efa in her kaleidoscope of hippy skirts, Efa and Nain were not so different anymore, not so different at all now Efa was all grown up and Nain was dead. And I just got on with it, with make-believing it all away.

Dad had gone away to make a million. Dad had gone away to find Mam. Dad hadn't gone away at all, he was here at the kitchen table, listening to this music here, teaching me how to whistle.

"How was the party?" Efa asks me after The Cuban Song's finished.

"Iawn." I shrug off the question. "There was cake," I say after, to make it realistic. "Chocolate cake."

"You've had enough to eat then?" playing Mam.

"O," I say. I hadn't thought of that. "O yes," I say, to be realistic again. There'll be the fridge in the middle of the night. It'll be a cheese sandwich. With mustard. I like mustard now, after trying it again with Pigeon. It's hot and tasty once you get used to it, mustard. My belly's grumbling when I think of the sandwich and all that butter and cheese. It'll have to wait until Efa's in bed.

Efa goes up to her room to 'have some space'. She does that more now. All the time she does it more. She's sick of me. Although it isn't my fault. Is it? It isn't *my* fault, The Home.

But tonight it's a good thing Efa wants 'her space' cos of the sandwich, and cos I want to think about Gwyn, and Pigeon. I get the bread out, and make a sandwich on the top in the kitchen with lots of spicy mustard and some tomatoes too. White bread. Butter. Cheese.

I hold it in two hands and take it up the wooden staircase to my room in the loft, next to Efa's. There's just a thin bit of wood between our two rooms. There, is Efa's 'space' on one side and here, here is my room. Nain and Dad had each slept at different times in the big downstairs room, and the most comfortable bed is there, and now it's empty, but neither Efa nor me want to sleep there yet.

"Don't come in!" shouts Efa in a cross voice when I pass her door.

"I'm not," I say. I'm not going in, I think.

Why's Efa so cross all the time? In my room I watch her through the slit in the wall, watch my sister in there in front of the mirror. Efa's scarves and beads and colours are all taken off, and there's just plain Efa sitting in front of her mirror in her white bra now. Thoughts go across Efa's face. She looks at herself in the mirror, Efa, and she's not happy with what she sees. She goes right up to the mirror then, pushes the skin under her eyes across her cheeks so her bags go smooth. It's because she's getting older and working too hard. Efa always says her face is getting ugly cos of The Home, although it isn't, it isn't ugly, Efa's face. Then Efa sighs and gets her packet of pills again. She stuffs a smooth tablet into her mouth. The pills are because of The Home and because of me. The pills and the yoga are for making Efa feel better.

When Efa looks in the mirror again, there's something in my sister's tired eyes makes me feel like I'm back on the bus with Pigeon, going towards that red cross. There's something in Efa's eyes that's like big weather. Angry. I look away.

I sit on the bed. The cheese sandwich is tangy and spicy and good; it fills my belly until it's satisfied, like a sleepy cat.

10

He had it all mapped out in his head. It was going to be like one of those adventure books they had in the school library, where children can be heroes and can change things for real.

"It's a five-stage plan," said Pigeon to Iola like James Bond.

He communicated the plan to Iola between cigarettes – puffing and coughing and exhaling clouds of smoke into the cobwebbed air of the attic:

First. Pre-pa-ra-tion.

They would need: a walkie talkie. A copy of the plan each (not to be forgotten or lost). And lots of practice.

Second. Dis-trac-tion.

Iola was to feign an allergic reaction to the ice cream. It was like they'd seen on TV. What happened to some people when they ate peanuts. For some people, when they ate peanuts they swelled up, couldn't breathe, turned red, shook like a storm. Iola was to hold her breath and shiver all over. So that...

Third. In-fil-tra-tion.

While everyone was distracted by Iola, Pigeon was to get in the van to spy on Gwyn.

"But…" said Iola. "But…"

Pigeon swatted her doubts away with more smoke.

Fourth. Comm-un-i-ca-tion.

Pigeon was to contact Iola from the van, and inform her of Gwyn's mis-de-mean-ours. i.e. what exactly it was Gwyn was doing wrong.

"What *is* he doing wrong?" asked Iola at this point.

Pigeon looked at her in disbelief "Do you really have to ask?" he said.

She shook her head. Of course not. Of course she didn't.

Fifth. Chase.

Iola, police in tow, was to chase Gwyn down.

"But," she said. "How come?"

"How come what?"

"How come the police are there?"

"You phone them, silly."

"O," she said. She looked doubtful.

Sixth. Inevitable success and locking up of the villain.

They were both happy with that.

The only trouble, was that Iola seemed unable, quite…

First. To understand what an allergic reaction really involved, and…

Second. To remember with any reliability the exact order of the plan.

But still.

11

Sunday. Sunday. Sunday.

I'm sitting with Pigeon in our living room. The sound of Gwyn's van drifts up the road, the pied piper songs of it lifting slowly up the hill, along the higgledy streets, and through the single pane of our living room window. Inside, me and Pigeon have been planning with a bit of paper. Pigeon has a pencil behind his ear and, with his black cheekbone from Him, he looks like he means business, so when I hear the van coming up the hill singing 'bla bla bla' and something about love or something, my bol lurches: hunger and nerves.

Me and Pigeon jump up from the sofa. Running out the door, I have that feeling like a held breath, like I always have when Pigeon thinks too much, because the best ideas are the worst too. There's kids coming from all the houses, Gwyn's off-balance songs pushing the children out of their doors like Efa's pills come through the shiny silver paper when you push on the plastic bubbles behind: Pop! Come the kids out of the houses. Pigeon and me race.

We're between the walls of the alley, climbing the fence at the end of it and running across the tarmac towards the van. Our shoes are hard on the road as we run up to the slot in the van's side and bend there, to pant as always. Our breath steams, the cold air white with it, and above us clouds sweep past, rolling over and over, heavy with hail.

In the slot is Gwyn's round face. Gwyn, smiling. He's looking down at Pigeon through the slot. The thick eyebrows. The dark eyes. The tanned skin.

"Iawn, bois?"

Together breathing "Iawn," in reply.

Pigeon's drawing up to the slot first, smiling at Gwyn. I back off, a few meters from the van. I can hear Gwyn laughing his bristly laugh, but the sound scatters on the wind like all the dust that was left of Nain when Efa threw her out over the town from the top of the hill. Behind Gwyn's van the mountains sit in twisting shapes, making zig zag lines against the sky, and the clouds make shapes too, like they always do. The high clouds are white sheets billowed up by the wind. The lower clouds hang like beards over the mountains.

Pigeon's talking now. His body moves with the words he says, pecking at the words like a bird feeding. Pigeon's talking a long time. He speaks in a long ribbon, pushing words into the cracks of the plan, waving his arms to push them in. In his one hand he's got one of His cigarettes, which he's kept like the money and the tickets and the receipts, and in his other there's an orange lolly now too, and now a chocolate one, and he's pointing at me, and I'm waving at Gwyn as if I'm on a boat going out to sea. Gwyn and Pigeon seem miles away from me. I'm all on my own, three metres away is like a different country, like China, or the United States of America or Spain.

Pigeon comes over to me, shoves the chocolate one into my hand with a look that means "C'mon!" and walks back to chat to Gwyn. I begin to unwrap, lick once, twice, heart beating.

Then I begin it, the riaction alergick we've been practising by Pigeon strangling me over and over against the rough stones of the school wall. I'm grabbing my own neck and wriggling on the ground like a worm out of the soil, pretending I can't breathe, going red in the face like Pigeon taught me.

I've never seen Gwyn's legs before: thick and short, wrapped in blue trousers and covered with a grubby plastic apron that has pictures of toy cars all over. The legs, and the dirty trainers at the bottom of it all, are running towards me. Through my bunched-up eyes, I can see Pigeon slipping into the van behind Gwyn's legs and behind all the other kids' faces looking at me as if I'm on the televison. Behind all this Pigeon just slides round the corner into the van like one of Efa's silk scarves when it runs through your fingers.

Now I'm getting my face back to normal, clearing my throat like a car starting, and beginning to nod to Gwyn that it's all right. He sits me up. His arm's round my shoulder, a killer's arm, heavy. Gwyn smells of dirty clothes, cigarettes, and sweat.

"I'm ok. I'm ok. I'm ok."

I'm saying it, over and over. But Gwyn doesn't believe me. Gwyn's face is covered with drops of sweat, like dew on a window. His breathing's fast and short. He's weird and worried, and, although I'm on my feet now, brushing myself off, Gwyn's still trying to get me to "ista lawr" to "relacs" and take it easy. He won't take no for an answer, Gwyn, and he's all worked up, and I don't get it. Why?

Five minutes later, I'm stood on my front doorstep, Gwyn's hands heavy and hairy on my shoulders and Efa looking down at me, eyebrows climbing up her forehead. Efa looks pretty fearsome stood there in all her flower-power glory. She's facing Gwyn down, shaking her head like the terminator, and she has that face she makes for men that says "you arsehole".

"Your daughter," begins Gwyn in his funny chapel Welsh.

"She's my sister." Frowning even more.

"Your *sister* has had an ALLERGIC REACTION. Perhaps indeed..." again his funny bible language, "perhaps indeed she needs to go to the HOSPITAL?" says Gwyn to Efa. He talks funny, like chapel, but with English in. Like as if he's learnt it. Like as if he doesn't belong.

Efa looks at me. I smile. Efa looks at me again, scowls at Gwyn. "Sothach!" she says quickly. *Rubbish!* And pulls me inside.

So that's that for my ice cream. And I'm sitting on my bed in the attic, upset about that, and about not seeing Pigeon, and not going out for all of today Efa says, pulling the two sides of her forehead together all cross like she's buttoning it up that long line between her eyes.

Now I'm frowning just like Efa, sitting on the bed, when I hear Gwyn's van starting up its tunes again, and I jump up, and my heart goes all over my body and into my head until it's full of a quiet thud and I go all cold with the feeling.

I'm looking into the window and the picture it makes, with the houses and the hill and the mountains past it, and, in the middle, trickling down the picture, is Gwyn's van, driving down and down, with a pop song that's like crying left behind a bit in the air as it goes away. It doesn't last long the song in the air and then all I can hear is the still house all around me, and past that, there's nothing but houses and streets and hills and trees.

"Psychological! Torturer! Murdrer!" Cher pushes, past Efa, past the door, and up the stairs. She's sniffing for air through all the crying she's doing, as if it smells to breathe. But I don't feel like laughing at Cher any more. Pigeon's gone.

Now we're face-to-face in the attic, closer than I've ever been to Cher. Cher's very pretty. She also actually smells really nice, like open windows and fresh grass. But she's crying, and saying "He's taken him! Murdrer, sicko, torturer! He's got Pijin!" although I'm telling her she's "got it all the wrong way round" like as if Pigeon isn't Pigeon and doesn't have good ideas, and like Pigeon isn't "cleverer than Gwyn and you and me and everyone else. Pigeon's the one that got in the van himself. Pigeon's the one."

But Cher just says, "Same difference, stewpit," and just when I'm starting to think a bit that Cher might be right and maybe Pigeon's dead and Gwyn = murderer so Pigeon = gone forever; just then I remember the plan.

The brown bits of Cher's eyes are two perfect rounds done with a compass and a sharp pencil when I tell her what we've to do next. While I'm talking I'm thinking Cher's so perfect and Cher's got the most perfect white skin I've ever seen, so smooth and pale it's like candles.

Then Cher and me are out, with Efa running out the door behind us shouting, "Where the bloody hell are you off to?" her shout dangling in the air as we speed down the hill on our bikes, coats spread out with the wind, making two coloured flags against the grey of the hill the pebble dash and the tarmac.

Pedalling, I see Gwyn's van ahead of us, at the bottom of the hill, where I always used to look left and right with Nain when we walked to school. I watch what the van does at the junction.

To the right is the road that goes down town. One grey, ugly road, and all the closed shops and the big kids and chewing gum on the floor on it, and Spar on it too, and at Spar that noise like dying they call 'mosquito', like a siren to keep kids out.

To the left is the way to the sea, and also to the left today a big sign for the fair and that's where Gwyn's van goes, with Pigeon in it. The van goes left. It goes quick, and me and Cher are following slow.

On our bikes we follow the van round the corner to the fair. The short winter day has almost run out like a battery now, and I'm tired, breathing really hard. My legs are burning with all the effort of pedalling, and hunger's making a big coil inside me.

When we reach it, the lights of the fair are like fluorescent pens already, although it's only just getting dark. The lights scribble and shine as they whirl, and the rides make the worst noise. There's people screaming everywhere like in 'hell!' up and down and round on the big rides. The screaming's spooky, considering what we know about Gwyn. Shooting games are everywhere too, which feels a bit weird too, considering.

Me and Cher leave our bikes by the chip van, all tied up to a lampost, and then Cher holds my hand. Cher is stiff and cold against me, and she's walking fast like when Efa stomps along in a mood. Cher takes this whole thing too serious.

We have to go round half the fair, feeling small between the people, the rides, the stalls, before we finally find Gwyn's van parked above a steep grassy bank that goes down and down, like for perfect sledging even without snow. The van looks like EddieTheEagle at the top of that bank. For the fair they've put plastic barriers all round the top of the slope, in case people roll down the bank. Past the barriers, the dark hill goes all the way down to the road by the sea below. The sea's turning black like the sky now, but you can still see the worm of the road below the fair, and the stripes of a zebra-crossing far below, and then the grey water stretching away into nothing.

Up here, the sign saying 'Hufen Iâ Gwyn's Ice Creams' stands like a castle's flag above the round heads of the people. A long tail of kids goes round to the slot in the van's side, where Gwyn's bristling face sticks out, smiling. He's busy getting the kids ice creams in all the colours they want. He recognises me, and Cher too, and he waves, but he looks at me like I'm trouble because of the riaction.

Where's Pigeon? Where's Pigeon? Behind Gwyn you can see there's a door inside the van, and maybe it's a toilet? And maybe Pigeon's in there, maybe that's where he is?

"Murdrer, murdrer. He's killed Pijin. Murdrer!" Suddenly Cher's screaming and kicking the side of the van. I want to stop her, but I'm too shy in front of the big kids in the queue and so I just say, "Don't be stupid, Cher, don't be daft", over and again. Cher ignores me and just keeps going.

"Murdrer. Murdrer!" she screams, and I know now why Pigeon keeps her out of his shed.

In the slot, Gwyn looks at Cher slow. He's frowning, doing a job at looking innocent. Behind him, kids on The Twister scream and whirl round in the air. Some of the big kids licking ice creams are laughing at Cher and one boy puts on a girl's voice and runs round in circles screaming "Murdrer! Murdrer!" while his mates cackle like gulls so that I'm all red now, and embarrassed. Pigeon was right about Cher. Cher's a pain.

"Don't be stupid, Cher. Don't be daft," I say again, all quiet, feeling sick as usual.

Cher doesn't stop, and the big kids are laughing more now,

so I get a hold of Cher's arms, trying to keep her back. It's like trying to hold back a dog that's swimming, Cher's arms and legs scratching and everything.

Then, behind and through everything, there's a shape, moving like a cat out of the van, past the sign on the side that says *Mind that child,* and running down the bank below, off into the dark. Pigeon's gone before Gwyn and Cher can turn round to see him. He disappears into the dark, like the smoke from his cigarettes disappears up to the black sky from his attic window. Then he's gone. Gone.

Watching him, my hands have stopped holding Cher and so she's running round the side of the van, pulling open the back doors. Cher's pink coat's flicking under the lights and my feet go smack and smack, hard and fast on the ground behind her, cos I hate being second most of all, even with Pigeon gone.

But now Cher's gone too far. Too far. She's jumped into the van with Gwyn and he's saying "Get out! Get out! You can't come in here!" and I stop. I stop.

And then it all happens quick. Like a flash Cher's fighting Gwyn's short legs. Like a tiger she is. And she's so sudden that she takes him down. Gwyn's falling hard against the floor of the van. His square body's heavy when it falls. And it's then the van suddenly shudders, and, watching, I get a panic feeling all fast like electric going up from my feet and to the start of my hair so it tingles and makes me hot and frozen.

I stand very still but the van isn't still, not anymore. It moves. It moves a bit, and where it is there's not such a slope and I think maybe I can stop it? And I think maybe the big kids not laughing anymore will stop it? And now it's down the bank, down, straight through the fence, and down and the wheels rolling. The wheels are rolling and through the back doors I can see Gwyn inside. His face is red, bristly, ugly, scared, and he's trying to get up against the angle of the floor, and Cher's inside too. Cher's inside too. Cher's screaming now inside the van while it goes. Cher's screaming. The van's rolling away and Gwyn's trying to jump out, and he's pushing and pushing with his legs out the door and onto the bank, shouting and pushing and falling to the ground. But Cher's inside. The van's going away. The van's going. That's all. That's all.

People are shouting all round me, pushing and shoving. I'm pushed about like a crow in the wind. I'm crying, and I'm cross I'm crying, hot drips, like the prissy hogan Pigeon says I am. I've seen kids doing this in fairgrounds before, that lost look, turning and turning on the spot. Stupid. And all alone. And now *I'm* like them: lost. Because I've lost Pigeon, lost Cher, and I'm standing in the fairground between the people all alone.

Now I collect worried women around me like flies on a dead body. Fags going droop from their hands, they're bending down to me, itching me with it's alrights from lipstick mouths.

And then, there's Efa! Breathing like she's been running, covered in scarves and trinkets with threads and bells hanging off her all over, she's coming towards me. I run to her, pushing everyone and everything away, because I want to smell Efa's salty skin, feel her arms, her breath rising and falling like the sea. And then. Efa's been crying.

And I see it now, and everything in my head goes quiet and smothered. When I look down the bank, and down to the road by the sea, between the dull white and black of the crossing far below, there's the van. There's arrows of glass all round it, and, by the side of the van, there's Gwyn, kneeling on the floor on the crossing, on a white stripe, and he's pulling his coat over another thing on the floor, curled still like a chrysalis on the black stripe, with little cubes of glass all round it. It has a face, white like a lily, and a stain, red like a pommygranite, is spreading from it on to the ground on the road down there at the bottom of the hill.

And now, on the other side of the crossing, his skin the colour of bones, Pigeon, thin and small, stands, staring at his new sister on the ground under Gwyn's coat. And I look at him, and I think as hard as I can, try to think it like Cher would've thought it, for real, how we know now, for certain, about Gwyn.

12

Pigeon stares. In the fair, the dark gathering away from it all, the fairlights whirling, the van resting on its side at the bottom of the hill, and Cher lying there, her soft skin white, dotted like a tabbycat's coat, but with red. Pigeon looks at Cher, and thinks it's strange how it's all happened, thinks how Cher believed it all, every word, and he didn't, not deep down. Didn't deep down believe his own stories about Gwyn.

Pigeon looks at Gwyn there, his angular body shaking over Cher's fragile one as he tries to get her to wake up.

"Tyrd!" Gwyn says, over and over, come on...

wake up...

wake up…

Cher stirs, just slightly, so you think she might become herself again, and then is still. And Pigeon doesn't really think it, not in a proper real sort of a way, not in words and sentences and paragraphs which make sense. No. But in a kind of black-blue way he feels how it's His fault, His. And while the ambulance comes through the fair like just another ride, and Cher is slotted into the back of it, with all the tubes and regular sounds and machines, Pigeon watches, and is angry.

To the side of the ambulance Iola's bright red coat runs down the hill, pulling away from all the people who hold her back and, when Iola runs through the ice cream and up to Gwyn, and kicks Gwyn, screams at him and shouts and shouts these make-believe can't-believe make-believe words: "murderer, murderer, murderer," Pigeon knows. He knows that he doesn't believe it, any of it, even that first idea, Gwyn = od. For that moment, just that moment, it comes tumbling down, the feeling, of hating Gwyn so much it can cover and hide and shelter the hatred Pigeon has for Him. Pigeon sees it all as it is, for that moment. And so Pigeon walks up to Iola, and, as he walks, lifts a hand up, and then smacks Iola right across the face.

Iola stops dead. She looks at Pigeon, looks at Gwyn, who stares at them both with red, scared eyes, and then she backs off into Efa's arms. Efa who stands looking at Pigeon hard, with that look they all give him, that look that says *that boy*.

The ambulanceman asks him does he want to come in with the girl? Pigeon shakes his head, says, "No. I'll be getting back now."

"Back where?" the man asks him.

"To my mam," says Pigeon. He shuffles off, his hands in his pockets, turning his back on the ambulanceman and his raised eyebrow, leaving Efa and Iola to answer the questions, thinking how he better get some clothes and things together quick, before He finds out about Cher and all the spilt blood and ice cream, before He gets wind of it, and before His rage about it all begins. The ambulance starts up and takes Cher off across the night, and Pigeon walks away, fading greyly into the crowds of the fair, where, except for the ice-cream van, and the police around it, everything slowly begins to speed and scream again as the rides quicken and beat once more under the moving lights, sped on by brusque, tumbleweed fairmen, with cash-belts at their waists and home strapped, like this fair, to their travelling backs.

And so it's night, black night, when Pigeon gets back up to the top of the hill, pushing and pushing the pedals of Cher's bike and his legs burning, and when he moves silently past his house and into the garden, and then into his shed, and gets his dirty grey schoolbag filled up with clothes, and takes his sleeping bag and an orange he's kept there, and that tenner he stole from Him last week, and a packet of His cigarettes, and he goes out again into the night, across the neighbours' gardens to find that old, ruined row of cottages, by the quarry, which are filled with nothing but the feeling of the dead hillside, where he's going to sleep tonight, safe from Him.

Pigeon curls up there, in the old quarry barracks, where the ruined slate huts are open to the wind and rain. Pigeon sits, thinking how the hut where he sits is like a skull, with holes for its window eyes. He sits, in his sleeping bag, waits for morning, and sleeps some, propped against the old hearth, used to the cold. He sleeps, far from the shed, from the house. But still the spectre of the house throws its long cold shadow over Pigeon.

Back in town, while the boy sleeps across the valley in that skull of a hut, He pushes Pigeon's mam in through their front door, pushes her so hard that her body tumbles and smacks like a dusty rug hit against a wall. And He shouts, "It's that sonofabitch," as He does it. "That sonofabitch's half killed her, god damn him."

And then, "Pigeon! Pigeon! Pigeon!" Until the house moves with His voice.

Pigeon's mam lies on the floor, waiting, glad for the stillness all round her, remembering a time, when she was eight years old, when she had found a little chick, fallen or lost from its nest, and she had tried to save it, and it had died in a cardboard box full of broken paper.

All the time she lies there, while He rants and rants, where is Pigeon? Where is Pigeon? Pigeon moves in and out of sleep in the ruined barracks, shivering with smallness.

It isn't until two days later that Pigeon ventures back to the crooked house, to tiptoe round the outside, peer in the uncovered window and see his mam sitting on the threadbare sofa, her face marked with sunshine and stormclouds and a bottle gripped in her hand as she rocks and rocks.

She looks up, sees him from the window. Stands.

Through the window she shouts. She shouts in that crazed

way of shouting that people who have no words for real conversation have.

"He's gone!" she shouts "He's gone, Pigeon!"

Pigeon stands. Still on the wrong side of the window. Looking into his house as if he's looking underwater at some deep pool barely penetrated by sunlight. He stands and he looks at her. It's hope, in her face. Hope and almost belief.

He considers going in. But Pigeon knows, knows it isn't that easy, Pigeon knows He'll be back, whether Cher comes with him or not. And then things will be worse, worse for his mam than before. Because He always comes back. He always does.

Pigeon goes to the shed, and sits on his bed in the pitch dark. And he thinks.

In the shed there are thoughts and ideas swimming and swimming up around him, and he can make no sense of them, make no sense of the stories that come into the shed in no particular order, as if they're lost, and the words and their meanings and where they belong in sentences and paragraphs are nothing to do with the sounds and shapes they make, there in the shed, in the pitch black.

Stories and words, they're useless if you can't do something, can't step up with the right word in its place, and use it, to hit, to hurt, to kill.

Pigeon shifted on the bed. Staring straight ahead of him into the darkness where only the faintest of shadows was thrown into the shed by the dim house. The dark was velveteen. His. A place to put anger. The darkness was a refuge. Pigeon sat, surrounded by black rage.

He'd got this far with the ideas, the stories, telling them to Iola and Cher so that they grew and grew and made things different, made Gwyn something else and changed things. But still it happened. Still those things continued to happen to his mam, and to him. And there was nothing the words could do to stop them. The words put up complicated defences, made arguments to and for. But that wasn't what you needed when He came, violent and ugly to the shed. You didn't need words. It was fists you needed. You needed to be able to fight it, and to see its face, and to kill it.

But he couldn't. Pigeon couldn't. And in he goes to the drawer in the house, and he finds it, wrapped in brown paper. It's His. It's hard and cold. It's violent and still. It's like a sleeping animal. Pigeon wants to use it on Him. He wants to use it, like wanting to breathe. But Pigeon can only put it back in the drawer.

13

Cher still hasn't come home. We don't go to see her. We're not allowed. But the town's slowly turning toward the sun again. The town heads into spring, day by day, into the thick of it. And Pigeon and me are obsessed with paper, with trying to understand things with paper and black words on paper, the black, twiggy print of words, on paper that's white as snow, the words so clear, and things making sense. Almost. We collect all kinds of 'documentation'. Pigeon says none of it makes sense. Pigeon says Gwyn doesn't makes sense. Then he starts saying I don't make sense either. He says it at me in an angry voice.

"You aren't true Iola," he says "You aren't true."

"What do you mean Pigeon?"

Pigeon says it then. "There's something in your family that doesn't make sense."

"What d'you mean Pigeon?"

"There's something missing," he says.

There's a piece of me missing. I nod. He's right. There are two pieces missing.

My dad.

And my taid.

Two men. The two men of my family. The two men that made *It's a world unfair for women, love.* Made Nain say it again and again so it stuck to you like glue.

"Have you looked for the answers?" asks Pigeon. He says, his eyes green and hungry for information.

"What d'you mean?" I ask him. How do you look for pieces of people? How do you look for the missing parts of a story?

"Paper," says Pigeon, "Look for paper."

So I look through Efa's box for letters, things to collect and read, like Pigeon would.

In the box there's mostly Christmas cards and boring things like Happy Birthday cards which are all the same and pointless but you have to pretend to like them. It's all like that, all the way down through the box, until almost the bottom.

And then I get a hold of it. All reeled up in elastic bands. A stack of postcards. When you look at the writing they're all from the same person. Who are they from? I've never seen them before. I don't recognise the writing. It's scrawny, jagged. Someone wrote the cards slowly, someone who isn't used to writing at all.

Every postcard has only one line, it says something like 'Today I am feeling better, I hope you're well.' Or 'Not such a good day today. Hope all is well.' Or 'How are things? Not a bad day today?' And then there's one that says 'Hope Iola's well.'

They're from Llanfairfechan according to the post-office mark. Why would you bother sending a postcard from Llanfairfechan? It's only a little bit away in the car.

And who is this person? Who are they from? The person doesn't sign them, just a kiss at the bottom.

Then I get to a new set, they've got a later date. 1990.

That's just last year. The year Nain died. The year it says on her grave. I take the elastic off them.

The first one is the same. Except. It's not. There's a name. It's not a name. It's Dad.

Dad.

I sit in the room, staring at the postcard. The room around me's still. Dad wrote to Efa. When? When? I look through the pile. This is the last date. I go to the window. Down in the garden there's still the strange bodies Dad had made all those years ago, metal and wood, warped by the rain, covered in bindweed, but still there.

Pigeon was right.

In the house downstairs there's the sound of Efa coming in, back from The Home. She's coming upstairs.

"Iola, be ti'n gneud?" asks Efa, standing in the doorway of the room now, seeing all the piles of papers I'm making. Her voice is far away.

"Where is he?" I ask her "Where is our dad?"

Efa's quiet. She's looking at her hands. She comes to sit down. She sits there a long time. Thinking of what to say. I'm holding the postcards like a shield between us. My sister lied to me. Efa lied.

"All Nain would say was 'He's left us, love. He's left us.'" she says after a long while "It wasn't until later she told me our dad was ill."

I sit on our sofa, next to her, listening for more.

"It was a few years before we began to visit him on a Friday. I don't know why Nain decided to take me. I remember we just went, and Nain didn't say where we were going. He was in Llanfairfechan, on a ward there, with four other men." She half smiles, but it's a sad, scared smile, "When we walked in, I could tell Nain'd been there before. She just walked straight across the ward, sat herself down by his bed, and got her embroidery out of her bag. I remember she was doing this little pink pattern with flowers on it." Efa's voice crumples like burning paper. I don't understand. What does she mean sick? What does she mean? I just wait for more.

"I remember those flowers, they were so perfect." You can hear the crossness in Efa's voice. So cross it's like the smell of burning. It makes you want to leave the room.

"It took me a minute to realise it was Dad. He sat there on the bed, and watched television as if we weren't there. He looked the same, but less thin. But he wasn't there, Iola." Her voice cuts off. Because she's crying. Efa's crying.

"He wasn't there." She's sobbing. Efa? "I tried to hold his hand, but he wouldn't hold back." She stops again. Watching her. I think it, for the first time ever, Efa had been quite young back then. Just a kid like me.

"We went every Friday, when you were at school. Sometimes I remember he'd look at me, and it was as if he'd seen me somewhere before, but he couldn't remember. And Nain'd just say, 'He can't remember, love', in this hard voice, not looking at him, still stitching the flowers on her bit of cloth. I started to hate him more than I hated Nain." That burning smell again, bitter and so strong I can't breathe.

There's a silence.

"What's wrong with him?"

"He was sick."

"What d'you mean."

"He was mentally sick."

Men-tal-ly.

"In the head?"

"Yes."

"Crazy."

"No," she says, and then she looks at me and says, "Yes."

Crazy is when you're dreaming even when you're awake. Crazy is when you can't keep things in order, can't hold days and nights apart. I consider it. Dad. I look outside at the wiry, stooping shapes in the garden. They were always just keeping us company, but now, looking at them, they look frightening, like zombies. Crazy. I think of the chicken meat he'd packaged up at the factory, all sucked of air. Crazy.

"Why didn't you tell me?"

Efa sighs.

"I don't really know," she says. "I didn't want you to ever sit by that bed, with Nain and those flowers, and with him looking at you as if, perhaps, he'd seen you before."

I don't understand her. I don't understand all of this story. Why not tell me? Why not. I needed him. I feel it, the big heavy thing around my ribs. Grief Nain called it. Grief. Grief is being so angry. So angry. Dad is alive, and sick and I need him. Dad was alive all this time and they knew where he was. They told me lies. They told me lies. Hot salty tears down my cheeks. Raggy, sore breathing. My shoulders are shaking. I'm shaking. Efa's hug is like a mother. Warm. The burning turns to her Patchuli scent.

"Where is he now?" I ask Efa.

"He lives just outside Liverpool," she says, "In a hostel. We can write to him. Maybe go to see him if you like?"

I stare at her. Efa. My sister, my mother, my dad, my everything. Then I look out at the shapes in the garden. The unforgettable wooden men who even the wind and rain haven't washed away, standing still in the garden, warped and stooping, cruel.

"No," I say. "No, I don't want to see him. Not now. Not ever." I run upstairs to my room. I throw myself on the cold bed, bury my face in the empty sheets.

I don't tell Pigeon. And I stop looking through the papers right then and there. If this is one of the pieces that's missing then stuff the other piece. I don't want Taid. I don't want the whole story to be so ugly. I'd rather be in bits. Because even when we find the missing stories, there's nothing Pigeon or me can do about it. We can't do anything about Him or about Dad, or about Efa or Nain or any of it. Except.

14

Gwyn Gelataio, son of Meurig and Mrs Gelataio, can't remember there ever being anything else but the flowers, sitting on the coffee table in his front room. The air in the room is stale. The plastic flowers sit in the stale air in a little pot in the middle of the coffee table. Everything is beige in the room; the sofa, the armchairs, cushions, the carpet and curtains, but the flowers, in their pot of foam, are shades of indigo and crimson. Gwyn can't remember there ever being anything else on the table, and has never considered changing this arrangement.

The pot and the flowers in it belonged to his late mother, Mrs Gelataio. Mrs Gelataio had been a devout Catholic. She was also tiny, Italian, extremely temperamental, and fond, with characteristic contrariness, of both the Rolling Stones and shrill tarantella, to both of which she would dance around her small kitchen in the port town, forgetting her prosthetic hip and high blood pressure, throwing her arms up in the air and laughing like a fresh bride.

Above all else she was fond of Gwyn. Proud of every hair that sprouted, wiry from his barrel chest, proud of his bulging belly, his lazy smile, and his legs "Shorta yesa, but astrong".

Finding a good woman for Gwyn, picking a nice girl from between all the dirty, drunk "English" ones in this Welsh seaside town, inviting a string of them home for tea ("no, acoffee") and organising for her son a stream of blind dates with the few girls who made it through the process of research, investigation, inspection and interview, had taken up between the hours of five and eight of every day since Mrs' Gelataio's weedy Methodist husband Meurig had finally given up and died, surrendering to a lung infection, and to his wife's desire to send him to purgatory.

Before he finally passed away, Meurig, in a long career as an ear-bashed doormat, had achieved three great successes of which he was justifiably proud. First, in a rare moment of adventurous spirit, taking his life's only ever holiday, to Tuscany, Meurig had returned with his small but impressive Italian bride and the accompanying commitment to a lifetime of earache.

The second achievement was to furnish his son Gwyn, through drilling and repetition just before bed, and through trips to Methodist Sunday School behind his wife's Catholic back, with a narrow but serviceable command of Welsh, excluding all swear words and including more than a fair share of biblical terms.

Thirdly, Meurig Gelataio (who had accepted his wife's olive oil and sunshine surname on their wedding day, quaking under a hard stare from her doting, scowling father) managed to protect his pot-bellied son from the worst of his wife's match-making tendencies for years, simply by providing her with the coarsest girls that his seaside town had to offer, complete with offspring and council flats, likings for shellsuits, "these aterrrrible plastic atracksuits", and ex-husbands behind bars.

So, when his father died, the world went into a frenzy of blind dates for Gwyn. At least once a week he was wheeled out, suited and booted, waxed and polished and adorned with his late father's fake gold watch, "You cannot atell, you cannot atell, and she willa like ita yes", a perfect side parting folding the black hair over his prematurely balding crown and enough money to pay him and the lady in question through a pub dinner "But aNO DRINK we willa not have a drinking girl."

And this was the problem. Never mind how nice, how amenable, how domestic, how full-figured these girls were, Gwyn's meek obedience to the no drinking rule, as he fetched first orange juice then tonic water then spring water for the ladies no matter what lambrinis, spritzers and cocktails they chose, was met with falling faces, eyes flicking to watches, and the abrupt need to go to the bathroom, to phone a friend, and to go home early.

Gwyn would arrive home to a tirade of questions. "So eeerly? So eeerly? Gwiiin but watt has ahappened tonite, you have acome home so eeerly! What is awrong with athese women, such a good man!" And then, taking his round head in her arms as Gwyn mumbled apologetically, she'd say, "It'sa all right my darrrling. So handsome! Your amother willa always love you, allllways."

Sue was the only woman who made it through the multiple stages of the selection process and through the dry first date. Sue was a capable, down-to-earth and dowdy girl, who must have been thirty but dressed to double her age, and was about as charming as a cold fried egg. But even Sue had informed him, a few weeks in, that she could never ever imagine living with Mrs Gelataio, and was quickly dismissed from the list with a snort, for the untiring process to begin again.

And if, when he sat on the sofa in his front room, Gwyn often thought of Sue, her thick plaid skirts, her cardigans, her bunned hair, and thought that it was a shame really that she had gone, it was only before he remembered meekly that he missed his mother more, for Mrs Gelataio had finally bowed out to an attack of angina whilst complaining about her late husband and pruning her long-suffering fig tree in the rare sun of last summer, going off to heaven via purgatory where poor Meurig had been sweating it out since his funeral two years previously, awaiting the arrival of his fierce little wife, and to be directed by her, up or down.

It was Gwyn's late mother who had dreamt up the ice-cream van. It was to be the unlikely vehicle for her son's social advancement since Mrs Gelataio had an exaggerated perception of the status of ice cream.

Gwyn awoke one Monday morning expecting a breakfast of pancetta and strong coffee, only to hear crazy ice-cream melodies blaring in the street outside, and, when he blearily opened the curtains, to find his mother standing proud and tiny next to the clash of new colours and posters and stickers that was 'Hufen Iâ Gwyn's Ice Creams' in all its brand spanking glory.

Mrs Gelataio, with her genealogical appreciation for fine ice cream, so concocted sweet icy delicacies, from dark sultry chocolate to basil and lime sorbet, only to be disappointed when the uneducated tonsils of the brats all along the coast and up into the yellow-grey hills opted for flakes, feasts, calypsos, and other such "abritish arubbish alollipop".

"These apeople are amad," she muttered, and the belief was further confirmed when, doubtfully sending Gwyn and the van out to a cold autumn fairground, it was found that the sales of ice creams, on that frosty day, didn't flinch. "Craizy!" she said under her breath, patting Gwyn on the head as she counted the money onto the chequered tablecloth in the dark kitchen.

The van keeps Gwyn in just enough money to maintain his flat, his beige living room, and his stifling status quo. But Gwyn, with his brown skin, his tasty winter ice creams and his bizarre chapel Welsh; Gwyn doesn't belong.

"Ma' Gwyn yn od." The words are whispered after him, as the children lick their ice creams with pink tongues. Gwyn is 'od', funny, strange. Gwyn Gelataio will have to be re-born.

Today Gwyn sits in his front room, in the flat his father bought for him and his mother had painted and furnished. Gwyn has never learnt to cook, nor to iron, wash, clean, make love. His mother's doting eye had provided him with the generally comfortable and unchallenging presupposition, that there was no need; and even now, with the microwave, the drop-off-pick-up service at the launderette, Mrs Lewis who calls to clean like a whirling wind once a week, and a few copies of *Playboy* to play with, this idea has remained happily unchallenged.

Gwyn, who divides his time neatly in half between going out in the van and lying in bed, with a little flexibility in the schedule for eating and long breaks in the toilet, only sits in the front room every now and again, when he feels he should because it's the room referred to, by the few people who've visited over the years, as the 'stafell fyw'.

So, every once in a while, during the weekday ice-cream lull, Gwyn makes an effort to sit in the front room. Gwyn Gelataio sits on the sofa, looking at the crossword puzzle. He's brought it here to complete. It should only take a half hour or so. And that's plenty of living for the room to have earned its name.

He gratefully surrenders his crossword to the desire to go to the toilet, at around three thirty, shuffling across the beige carpet, through the door, across the hall and into the loo, locking the door against his mother's ghost, pulling his big blue jeans down over his white behind, and perching on the only seat in the flat over which he feels a sense of ownership, picking up in his square hands a magazine filled with girls and cars, both of which he covets, and relaxing slowly.

CLANK! From outside.

Gwyn's white behind lifts into the air a foot or so, and the magazine goes flying too. Running out of the toilet door, trying simultaneously to pull his trousers and paisley knickers up from around his ankles, rushing to the front room again, and pulling back the curtain a little, Gwyn, trousers still hanging at his knees, breaks out in a cold sweat.

The boy stands beside the little girl, pale, face to the window, catapult and stones in his hands, waiting.

"Agor y drws! AGOR Y DRWS!" the boy shouts, seeing Gwyn's round face wearing the curtains around it like a wig.

Gwyn quickly drops the curtains back over the window, terrified. Ignoring the children's demands to be let in, he tries to tiptoe across the room away from the window, a cumbersome undertaking for such a square body on such small little feet. He finally reaches the kitchen, closing the door tight and exhaling with relief against it.

In the kitchen are all the mod cons bought by Mrs Gelataio, a blue lino floor, some enduring plastic fruit in a bowl, and a photograph of herself, smiling like steel, which now stares down at Gwyn.

Gwyn has no idea what to do. Problem solving is not a forte. Children are his livelihood, flocking to his ice creams with their pences and pounds, but Gwyn has no idea how to negotiate with a child and no treats to offer, the fridge and the cupboards empty and his mind fogged by the increasingly pressing need to go to the bathroom.

He's still frozen against the kitchen door when a crash, followed by the sound of glass breaking heralds the arrival, colliding into the door just beside his hairy right arm, of a sharp grey stone.

Gwyn looks at the stone, and from it his eyes trace a trajectory to what was once the kitchen window. In place of the window, staring through the ragged hole is a small, white face.

It stares. Gwyn stares. The boy stares. Gwyn runs back through the door, across the beige carpet, past the plastic flowers, across the hallway and into the toilet again, locking the door behind him. Then he realises the whole thing was a bad idea.

Through the toilet door he can hear the sound of glass crunching, a girl and a boy's voices arguing, feet landing smack tinkle on the floor as they jump through the broken window, footsteps padding across the carpet and closer and closer and closer, up to the toilet door. Gwyn stands in the little toilet, just the toilet bowl looking up at him, the tiny frosted window open on its hinges as if half blinking uselessly at the street outside, his mother's can of air freshener, and the pile of magazines set there to get him through the boredom of constipation, and that's all.

"He's in the toilet," a girl's Welsh voice, shrill as metal.

A witchy boy's laugh.

"Tyrd allan, Gwyn!"

It's an order that Gwyn, cowering on the toilet seat, wouldn't think to obey.

The boy mocks him. "Scared of kids? Scared of kids are yer?" he scorns.

Gwyn's blood pressure climbs, in fear and shame.

The toilet seat creaks dangerously as Gwyn places a foot on either side of it and hoists himself up to take a look out of the window. The street's empty, the carefully cut lawns blank. There are no cars parked, no echoing arguments or irritating radios. Everyone's at work. Perspiration breaks out on his upper lip, and drips begin to roll down his forehead.

The boy tells the girl to "Ista lawr yn fana" and guard the toilet door. Gwyn can hear feet, probably the boy's, scuffing around the flat, can hear footsteps pacing across the hall and into the bedroom. Gwyn thinks of his mother's silver picture frame, his new TV in the bedroom that swells all the people to twice their usual size, thinks that he hasn't put *those* magazines away under the bed, hasn't made the bed in fact, or opened the curtains today. Gwyn blushes, standing on the toilet.

Gwyn, crouched on the toilet seat, can still hear whispering outside the door, and the girl's occasional sniffling, sitting low, the sniffing sound about halfway up the door. After a while, he decides to try talking to her.

"Sut mae?" says Gwyn shakily.

The sniffing quietens.

"Be ydach chi'n ei wneud yma?" His Welsh is even more formal than usual. Asking the question, there's the sinking feeling that he doesn't want to know why they're here after all.

There's a silence. A sniff. Then, "Dilyn fo."

And that's it. There it is. No answer, no reason, just follow my leader. That's the problem, for these children and for Gwyn: follow my leader. Gwyn knows that game well.

There's the sound of the boy running back down the stairs, of paper rustling, of the girl whispering fiercely to her friend, the boy not replying.

Then the corner of one of *those* magazines pokes under the door, followed by another and another, until the gap under the door is stuffed full of paper. Gwyn looks down at the magazines. Disembodied little breasts and bottoms. Lacy underwear. Pouting lips. Then there's a strange smell, of oil, or kerosene? A kind of scraping sound outside the door, the sound of feet receding away. It's not until the first whisp of smoke snakes under the door that Gwyn gets it. Like a rabbit in a hole.

Still Gwyn sits on the toilet, watching the smoke sucking under the door, loitering long enough for the flames to start licking the door, the sound of crackling to begin, the small toilet to fill with smoke. Gwyn hesitates just a second or two more, then starts clambering for the window, pushing his head out, and then his shoulder, and shouting and shouting for dear life. When he's halfway out, his fat legs hanging behind him over the toilet seat, he can feel the heat on his backside and flames licking at his ankles, because his other magazine pile, set by the toilet, with the cars, has begun to burn. And when Gwyn Gelataio tumbles to the damp grass outside he's a new-born-middle-aged-babe, his clothes blackened by the fire, the short little hairs on his ankles singed down to a sweet, curly stubble.

15

Afterwards, on the bus, counting the streets back home from Gwyn's, Iola's not speaking to him. She sits next to Pigeon, shaking.

"Stopia," he says. "Stopia."

"Sori," she says. And then, "Sori, Pigeon," again. She keeps shaking.

Pigeon turns away from her, stares out the window. It's started to rain. Wet rain. That's what they call it when it falls like this, heavy drops, full of sky.

"Bydd Gwyn yn iawn, Pigeon?" she asks him. Her eyes are big and blue and there are no ideas in her eyes. *Will Gwyn be alright?* She asks him, over and over. Will Gwyn be alright, Pigeon? Will Gwyn be alright?

"Falla," says Pigeon. He moves his shoulders for *Not sure*.

Pigeon should we go back? Should we go back, Pigeon?

"Na," he says. "Na."

It's not the kind of thing you can go back on anyway. In his pocket there's the box of matches. Only one left.

There's a crumpled cigarette in his pocket too. He'll have it when he gets back home. It's the last of His cigarettes.

Maybe the last cigarette Pigeon'll have for a while. Next to him, Iola's started to cry. Her nose drips with the tears.

She's too small. She's not helping anything. She has no ideas. Pigeon looks at her. She's useless to him. He gets up at the next stop. I'm going to walk from here, he says.

She looks at him, blue eyes. No idea. No idea what he means.

She tries to get off too. "Ddim fanma, Iola," he says. "Y nesa". *The next stop*, he says. Get off at the next one.

But she wants to come now, with him. She jumps off the bus after him, crying more. She can barely walk, with her untied shoelaces, and with her tears. She's crying so much there's snot coming from her nose. She's ugly. Hopeless.

Pigeon turns round to her. "I don't want you to come by mine again, or ask for stories or anything ok, Iola?"

Pigeon looks at her once. He feels nothing when he looks at her, as if she's just a piece of cardboard, or rubber, or wood. He turns and walks away and doesn't turn round, knowing she's standing in the road on her own in the rain.

He just wants to walk. He walks up the long, ugly hillside road, past the houses where there's people sitting down to dinner, watching TV. The streetlights are orange all over town when you look down at it from this hillside road. Downtown's small from up here, and nobody in it matters.

Pigeon walks up the hill, towards his house. There's nothing left to do but go home for him, home to the shed and his Mam, her dead dresses, and the dark quiet. Go home and wait for them to come.

Pigeon goes into his crooked house, his actual home, for the first time in months. Pigeon walks into the lounge, where his Mam's sitting under the lamp which she hasn't switched on. He sits with her in the darkness. Pigeon sits, and she rocks, and he tells her slowly what he's done, tells her as if she can understand.

"Dwi 'di brifo dyn, Mam," he tells her. "I've hurt a man." As if the words are worth something, as if they don't fall to pieces in the dead air.

"What d'you mean, love?" she asks. But he can only say it again.

"I've hurt him."

And he sits shaking. When he looks at her, all he sees is that she's afraid too. In the silence after the words, the silence that lasts for hours, Pigeon waits for it, for them to come take him away, punish him.

But He does instead. He comes home, crashing in through the door, angry and drunk and heavy as a stone, and He goes for her. But not for any new reason, and not because of Gwyn. He goes for her. Goes for her as she sits there rocking and He wants to kill her, He says it. Says it and doesn't mean it, just as Pigeon's heard Him say before. But she believes him, Pigeon's mam is screaming and begging him, so that it tears you apart.

Pigeon's thinking it'll be like this forever: Pigeon in the shed and his mam rocking and Him coming to keep breaking it all up. And Pigeon does it. He smacks Him full in the stomach. With the hit, which lands full and hard in the centre of His wide, strong waist, the whole room collapses down to just the two of them. Just the two of them. His mam runs out, away from, him, from Pigeon. And, in the room, it's just Him, and just Pigeon, and Pigeon's sore, useless fist. As for Him, he's winded. Doubled over, but f***ing and blinding, and he'll get his own back soon as he can stand straight again. One, two, three seconds.

Pigeon can't see a way out. Not even Gwyn and the fire have made it any better. There's still this feeling, like having his legs and arms bound, and like trying to breathe underwater. And Pigeon can't. He can't breathe.

Pigeon can't breathe, so he's across the room, opening the drawer, opening the drawer to get it out, holding it in his hands. It's cold and hard. It's violent. An animal stirring. Gasping for air, for the surface, Pigeon pushes the little catch away, like a dog baring its teeth.

16

The dark street's quiet, Sunday quiet, and there's just the orange lights along it, the sound of my feet walking, and, at the end of the street, the crooked house, and shouting penned in by walls.

So what if Pigeon told me on the bus after the fire at Gwyn's to get out of his stories? So what do I care? I start walking towards the crooked house after Pigeon. I'm in on this now, so I'm not just going home to Efa as if nothing's happened. And maybe it'll be alright. Maybe Gwyn got out, and maybe it'll be alright and Pigeon will want me back?

There's a light in the crooked house. I don't want to see Him so I go past the house, and down the garden towards the shed, and that's when they make sense, the noises. And that's when I know. I know what they are. I'm not stupid. I can hear Him shouting. And I can hear the sound of hitting. But most of all I can hear Pigeon. And maybe it's that. Maybe it's that, that crying that's like a kid, Pigeon crying like he's just a kid, that makes me know I have to get in the way of Him just so He stops. I'll make it happen myself.

I'm so quiet, and I move so carefully, it's like I'm not me. I'm not Iola. I'm someone better. Someone who knows exactly what to do. She's strong and careful and she moves up to the house, pushes open the door, hears His shouts, the sound of Pigeon crying, and then quiet. The room and what I'm seeing begins to make a picture.

There's Pigeon standing in the room, and there's Him holding Pigeon to the floor, and then I see it, Pigeon's holding it to His head.

17

Iola's gone, Pigeon goes to the gun, which lies on the floor beside Him. The gun's dead now, the power of it gone. The gun's just an object, just a thing Pigeon takes and wraps in brown paper again, and holds to his chest as he leaves the house, quickly by the front door.

He walks. He doesn't run. He walks calmly to the quarry, up between the old barracks where the men used to sleep, and then into the quarried hill, where slices have been cut from the mountains, like spoonfuls snatched from a cake. Pigeon walks, then clambers up to a small tunnel in the hillside, and crawls through the black passageway, toward the green, watery light on the other side. There, in the lost world of another quarry, hidden deep inside the hill, decorated with ferns, lichen, and gentle moss, Pigeon finds a long crack in the slate wall, and pushes the gun and its brown paper wrapping deep inside, as far as his arm will go into the dark, split slate.

When Pigeon arrives back from the quarry, wet to the skin since he wears no coat, and only his thin school trousers, it's calm in the house again. Sewing, Pigeon's mam hums a sea shanty under her hanging dresses in the dark of their unsteady house, and all around her the town sits down to meat, and television stories.

His mother looks up suddenly, stops singing.

"Pigeon?" she asks into the heaviness of the room. It's so dark in the lounge that it's not possible to see her working hands or the coloured thread, the bending fabric. She keeps sewing, diligently, mechanically.

Breathing short and tight, Pigeon moves closer.

"Help," he says, almost in a whisper. "Please, help."

They look at each other, the dim shapes of each other. She rocks. He goes to her, sits at her feet and puts his boy's face on her lap as she sways. She strokes his hair. They wait like that as she hums a song or two, until Pigeon hears a car outside and rises, kisses her soft, fading hair.

The car's coming for Pigeon, but not because of the fire at Gwyn's, or because of Him. No one has put two and two together yet, not put them together: Pigeon and the fire, Pigeon and the van, Pigeon and Him. The car's coming because it was coming anyway.

They had already been round the week before. Two had come to the crooked house, asking their questions. They'd heard Pigeon had bruises. They'd heard the man, the step-dad as they called Him, was a nasty piece of work. They'd heard Pigeon didn't go to school. They'd come round with a clipboard, asking questions.

"When was the last time you went to school, Pigeon?" they'd asked.

"Last week," Pigeon'd said. "We did English. And maths. We did mathematics." But his face was so narrow, and his eyes, they were darting, like a cat's.

"How did you get your bruises?"

"Fighting." Pigeon grinned at them.

"What about your mam's?"

"Fighting," Pigeon'd said, then he'd looked away, shrugged. "But not with me," he'd added, sulky.

"Who makes sure Pigeon is going to school?"

"Mam," said Pigeon "Mam."

And all the time Pigeon's mam rocked back and forth, back and forth.

His mother continues to rock this time, as they come up the path to take Pigeon away. This time it's two policemen and a woman.

From behind the cobwebs that are like a veil over the window, Pigeon watches the policemen get out of the chequered car, walk up the little path, speak into the tiny microphones on their chests. They wear heavy boots and padded waistcoats. They wear black, and little chequered bits on their sleeves: black and white checks, like a chessboard.

"Yep, we've found the house," one says into the little microphone. "Should be out in a half hour or so, keep you posted. Yep, Linda's with us, she'll do the talking."

Pigeon isn't afraid of them. It's the woman he doesn't like, he doesn't like the women who come with questions. He sits down in His chair in the living room, in the darkest corner.

No one answers the knock, so one of the officers pushes at the ragged door. As they move along the dark corridor towards him it's like turning the last page of a bad story.

In here Pigeon just sits in the dark. He sits in the threadbare armchair that's opposite his mother, rocking on her own chair. Pigeon's waiting for it. Waiting for them to make it real.

"Excuse me," says the woman, nervous at the door. And Pigeon's mam, she just rocks back and fore on the creaking chair holding her face where He hit her.

"Hello, Mari? Hello...Pigeon?" The woman is nervous, respectable, out of place in the dank room. Neither Pigeon nor his mam change position. Pigeon sits in the dark, cross legged on the armchair. His chin is in his hand, resting. He stares at the window, although the heavy curtains are closed. He's blank.

The woman peers in. Perhaps she can make out the shape of the boy sitting in the armchair, perhaps she sees the faint halo of his mother's white hair rocking back and forth in the chair. He can see just the outline of the woman's smile. She smiles in the way you smile at a child's impossible handwriting, struggling, struggling to understand, struggling to encourage.

"Excuse me, Mari," she says, trying a different tack, her voice a little high, a little strained.

"Don't speak to her, Mam." Pigeon's hard, pegged-down voice shoots across the room.

A sharp intake of breath. Then "Mari, do you remember what we talked about?" The woman's voice tinkles inappropriately in the room.

Pigeon's mother's white head moves back and forth, back and forth. There's silence. Silence except for the persistent creak and then a snorting sound from the corner: Pigeon's chuckle. His chuckle, like pulling a finger at them all.

One of the policemen takes a step forward.

"Afraid we've got to take him away, madam. We've no choice under the circumstances. He's at risk see? I'm afraid..." switching on the light.

The light falls on the brown armchairs, on the brown sofa,

on the full ashtray, on Mari's white head, on Pigeon's slight shoulders, on the dirty carpet and on Him.

He lies there, face down. There's a wound in the back of His head, a small black and red wound. There's a slick of blood on the floor. The light from the bare bulb makes shapes in the maroon blood. Pigeon watches the shapes with interest.

The light also falls on the woman's concerned face, which crumples like a vacuum-pack. And now the light is switched on, they will also see something new in Pigeon. He won't hide it.

Pride.

"Fi nath o," says Pigeon, pointing at Him, "Fi."

It was me. It was. It was me.

The words settle into his stomach, like something molten becoming stone.

18

It isn't chapel. It's church. Catholic. He was Catholic, Efa says, but I can't imagine Jesus with his sharing and his fish and his bread and his washing people's feet having anything to do with Him at all, chapel, church or anywhere. But anyway they have the funeral in the Catholic church in the town by the sea where Gwyn lived. We walk there from the bus stop, and we see the big black car going into the carpark by the church. We're wearing black again, like for Nain.

"There they are," says Efa when the big black car comes. "We're late," she says, grabbing my hand. We walk up the path and into the church in a hurry. The church is all pretty windows and smells that are like magic and pictures of fairytale people from the Bible.

At the funeral there are only fifteen people. There's me. There's Efa. There's Pigeon's mam. She looks a bit clearer than usual. Less blurred. But her eyes are as lost as ever. There are some men from His work. Men with big shoulders and heavy hands, who are bigger than Him and who look grim. They come in with Him. Carrying him. Looking like they want to start a fight as they hold up the heavy box.

"Bloody disgrace," says one of them, as he passes Pigeon's

mam, sitting at the front on her own. She shrinks like a spell, swallowing herself up, like a snail curling into its shell. Now you see her. Now you don't. I thought for a minute, when I first saw her, that she looked better, more there, but now she's smudged again, like rubbed-out pencil, with nothing to say.

The Bloody Disgrace is because of it being Pigeon. Pigeon who's been taken to the police station. Her son. When I look at her for long I start to feel cold and like I've got something wrong with me. Maybe my heart. My stomach. Maybe that.

Apart from that there's no one, except for me, Efa, and at the front, sitting in a chair with wheels, Cher. She sits there in front of a teenaged girl who's wheeling her about.

"Who's that?" I ask Efa.

"Cher's sister perhaps," says Efa.

That can't be right can it? Cher doesn't have a sister. She just has Pigeon and his mam and the crooked house.

"She's looking better," Efa says, "You should go over and say Hello," she says. But when I look at Cher I feel sick to my stomach so I just stand next to Efa and look at the coffin where He is, in that wooden box that's closed up like a fist. I imagine him inside it, scowling.

Adrian, they call Him. *Adrian*. It says His name on the front of the little booklet they gave us on the way in. *In Loving Memory of Adrian Macauley*. It's strange to see *Loving* anywhere near His name.

When the service starts, the priest talks about His life as if He was a boy once. As if He was like us, me and Pigeon. But He never was. No way He ever was.

"Adrian grew up in Liverpool," says the priest.

Liverpool. Where our dad lives now. I think about Dad, standing here with Efa. What would Dad think of all this. But

ALYS CONRAN

Dad's crazy. He can't think probably. He doesn't really exist. Like a dream person. Or angels. Or Pigeon's mam.

Adrian Macauley had four brothers and a sister according to the priest.

I feel sorry for the sister. She isn't here. Neither are the brothers. I bet they teased the sister and twisted her arm in a Chinese burn and were meaner than even Pigeon is to Cher. Bet He was mean. He was mean. He was mean. *He deserved everything he got*. But that thought is too big and too nasty. *Serve Him Right*. I can't think that either. Not properly.

"My impression," says the Priest, "is that he was a boy full of fun."

The priest talks about this Adrian and the games he used to play as a kid. Fishing. Tiddly-winks, which means counters, and boxing. That makes sense. Boxing. Adrian was never a kid. I know he wasn't. He was Him.

"Lets not beat about the bush," says the priest. "Adrian could knock out a man twice his size." The big men laugh. Pigeon's mum doesn't, she just sits there, being alone and small and pretty and *a Bloody Disgrace*. I look at her, feeling how Pigeon isn't there, where he should be, sitting next to her. Efa says not to mention him. "He's not allowed to come," she says. Like he ever would. Like he'd want to hear about this Adrian.

Standing in the church, looking at the coffin with Him in it, I think how it was Adrian. The massa-killer, the sicko-psycho, was Him all along, and I never knew. Pigeon never told me. I never knew until I saw Him in their living room that day, with Pigeon. Hurting Pigeon. My friend.

The hymns for Him are very quiet because there's only fifteen people. Some of them are the same songs we know in chapel, but they're in English instead in this church. Only the priest really sings. He sings nice and round into his microphone, and it's like he really believes in the song and in God! and in Him. And then the priest, who's dressed in a long robe like a warlock, with a scarf around his neck and a special serious look on his face shakes clouds of spicy smells over the coffin where He is, as if He's something that should be treated kindly, as if He's something special, as if He's something soft and not just a body you have to break to survive.

"What's the priest doing?" I whisper to Efa.

"He's blessing Adrian," she says.

"What's that?" I say, pointing at the swinging metal thing that the priest holds.

"Incense."

"What for?"

"For making the dead person special and holy."

"Him?!" I say it too loud and people turn round.

"Sh. Iola," she says. And the priest goes on shaking the spices and smoke all around the coffin, as if He is something you have to be kind to, and make charms for.

That's crazy, I think. Blessing *Adrian*.

Blessing Pigeon, that's what they should all be doing, blessing my friend, not this dead man in his box. Thinking that is so angry and dark I feel sick. I think about the holes in the body that's in the box. Straight through his body, and the blood. And then I can't breathe with the singing and the priest and the church and Cher, and with Pigeon not being here. It's like the church and me are full of holes and I'm leaking all the breath I try to breathe. I'm full of holes and Efa's holding me, and she's got me by the shoulders and she's pulled me outside.

"Sorry, Iola," she says, holding me to her warm body, as I shake and try to breathe. "This was a bad idea. I shouldn't have made you come."

She holds me, standing outside the church. She holds me until I stop shaking. We go for a hot chocolate in the National Milk Bar and I have mine with a flake and Efa's so kind to me I want her to love me like this forever and love me as if we'd never ever told each other any lies like that lie lying in that box in the Catholic Church. I want Efa to love me enough to make up for Dad, for Nain, and now for Pigeon, now for Pigeon too. I want her to love me so much it stops up all the gaps, all the bits where there should be love and there isn't. And after the hot chocolate, I cry. It's not that I cry for Him, for his funeral with its false magic spells and its one man singing on the microphone. I cry for Pigeon. I cry for Pigeon so much it's like tearing paper.

19

"I dunno. Snot really my problem. Snot really anythin' t'do with me."

The room is white, calm, hard, cold. Pigeon sits on a big leather chair. It's what they call an executive chair, and it's there for adults. There is a smaller chair in the room, one for children, but Pigeon has ignored the *Police Psychologist*, and he's sitting in the big chair, and so he's looking at her straight, eye to eye. There are also toys on the floor for kids. "To make it easier for children to talk," she says in English, with her smile like aluminium. But Pigeon isn't having any of that either. He sits on the chair, in the little white room. He sits perfectly still, facing her. She sits also, in her white shirt and her black trousers, her notebook, her hair pulled back. The room has a video camera, with a little light to show that it's filming. It's always filming. The room also has a panic button.

Looking at her like this you can see that he makes her uncomfortable. Her legs and her arms are crossing and uncrossing, crossing and uncrossing again and again all the time, as if she was the one on trial. This is how Pigeon's evidence will be given. From this room, locked away. Pigeon can go to the trial if he likes, but his evidence will be on camera.

"Fair enough!" she says, at his refusal to answer. She smiles like make-believe. "That's fair enough!"

She says the last fair enough as if it's on your marks, get set, go! But Pigeon doesn't start, he simply scowls.

"How about your dad?" the woman carries on with her endless nosy-poky-parker questions. Who is she to ask about his dad. Pigeon's dad doesn't exist.

Pigeon scowls more, and he says nothing. He throws one of the little bright plastic balls that are part of the toy box between his left hand, and his right hand, and then back again, from one hand to the other one, from one hand to the other. Pigeon tries it, to control the room, to bring it back under control. Pigeon copies what He would have done, controlling it by throwing that little ball from one hand to the other, one hand to the other. Pigeon's heart beats hard.

"Okaaaay," she says, pulling the okaaaaaay out like bubble gum. "How about your stepdad then? How did you two get on?"

And Pigeon hates it, the way 'you two' sounds. "He's gone," he snaps. "He's not around anymore anyways," and he lets the ball fall to the floor, watches it as it slows against the deep-pile carpet and finally stops against the skirting board, cornered.

"Hmm," she says. "Yes, I see. But were you friends?" and she leans forward, slightly. You can see it on her skin, the prickles of getting to the bottom of it, of unlocking the secrets. The prickles wander like ants up her arms.

Pigeon looks up, is still for a second, and then, "No! We weren't 'friends' alright?" And it's a man's anger, uncontainable in his boy's voice.

"If you don't want to talk about it Pigeon, then that's alright, okay? That's fine for today."

She shakes her head, shuffles her papers. She looks at him, almost kindly. Almost mothering. But the room is too white. And she isn't a mother. She isn't his mother.

"Yep, that's right." Pigeon rests his forehead in his hand. "Don't want to talk about it," he says, pursing his lips.

"Okay, fine, we'll do this some other time Pigeon, okay?" She looks at him a long while, her eybrows pulled down low.

But Pigeon doesn't want to do this ever again. Doesn't want to sit in this room with the stupid toys, the grinning bears, the shiny, ugly-perfect balls, the dolls and the cars and all the other things that adults need children to have, so he says suddenly, "I hated *his* guts," and then, "*He* spoilt everything. He was a bastard to mum, and a bastard to me."

"Who's H*e*?" She's looking confused, looking at her clipboard, as if she's lost her place on the page.

"*Him,*" Pigeon leans forward, with his own italics this time, reaches for her clipboard and taps his finger twice about halfway up the page.

Step.

Dad.

She flushes and makes a note, but Pigeon grabs her notebook halfway through.

– *difficult relationship – possibly repeated violence? – Psychological mistreatment? –*

"Pigeon, Give that back!" she says. You can hear the strain in her voice. Fear? Her upper lip sweats as he holds the notebook, reading with interest as the description of him grows across the page, her handwriting adding flesh to the bones, describing his pigeonhole to a T. But he gives her the notebook back, impatient to get out. To get away.

"So anyways, I did it. Might as well tell you. I did it."

"What?"

"Well, Gwyn's house for starters!" He shakes his head, almost laughs.

"Who's Gwyn?" Again she's confused, again looking in her papers for the answer, frowning.

Pigeon looks at her, and his eyebrows go up.

"Don't you know anything?" he asks her, as if interested. He smiles. He's enjoying this, except for the feeling; the feeling that The joke won't be worth the pain.

She shuffles through her papers, frantically looking for a note, a scribble, an underlined name.

"He's the ice-cream man," says Pigeon with a helpful smile. "I burnt down his house."

If it wasn't for that Pigeon might have got off lightly, even with the body lying in holes on the ground. He would have got off lightly because he had bruises, Pigeon, and his mam would testify that it was self-defence, and even His friends knew that *Adrian* was a brute. But burning that house. Burning Gwyn's house. That carried the boy into a different league. He was malicious. He was dangerous. He had to be locked up a good while. Re-educated. Spat out brand new.

20

We don't talk about it much, me and Efa. She doesn't ask me many questions. I don't ever ask her if she's glad Pigeon's gone. She doesn't think it's anything to do with me, so she doesn't ask. All the things they talk about at school, and at chapel and in the paper, they're nothing to do with us. It's just Pigeon's life. His life. So Efa goes on working at The Home, and doing yoga, and trying to make it all up to me, the lies she's told. But there's so much space between what we know and what we say now. However much we hug, we can't close the space. I think of him all the time, Pigeon. Someone to believe in. Think of the last time I saw him. The last time I had a real friend, someone close. As close as two crossed fingers.

I'd been hiding in this alley between the houses when the men came up the road to take Pigeon away, the men and the woman. So, when the men were at Pigeon's door, all in their uniforms, I could see Pigeon looking from the window, and I knew they wouldn't let him stay there, not in that dirty house on his own with his mam who'd got lost somehow, especially not after what he'd done. And the men were going in, pushing through the broken door, through all the rubbish in the hall. From behind the hedge I was scared about Pigeon, and where he'd go now. It was a deep, settling fear, like swallowing a cube of ice that never melts. And then a bit after, Pigeon came out and got into the car between two men, and the car went off down the hill and away, and then there was just me and the house and the hill.

All weekend it was I don't know. I don't know. I don't know anything. Then it was Monday with rain and tall teachers and school, and name-calling like knives as usual. Except now people were saying things about Pigeon. He'd killed his dad, they said. I wanted to scream at them for it. For that. Because it was a lie. He wasn't Pigeon's dad.

At school, in the new classroom out the back, in a kind of a caravan, with Ms Thomas blaring her screechy voice at the kids all day, I kept my head down. I said nothing. I kept my promise to him and I said nothing. I held my pencil tight in my hand. When the blunt nib of the pencil moved across the paper it was like the sound of ironing white sheets. It was a good sound. Regular.

And that was how it began. This writing and reading. It was Pigeon going, that was how my schoolbooks filled up with neat writing. Ticks and exclamation marks abracadabra'd at the bottom of homework. Efa got a shock at parent-teacher evening, seeing my writing filing away down the pages, like a good girl's, like Cher's before the accident.

I sat in class all quiet, the laughs and mutters, the sounds of all the other kids making a blur around me, and playing at the edges of me as if I was going to disappear. The teacher talking was like a TV you're not listening to. At break-time I sat in the corner, on the step, my knees pulled up to my chin, my pale hair falling onto them and round my face. With one hand I picked pebbles off the yard floor and scraped at the concrete with them, looking through my hair, drawing birds and hearts and houses.

After the funeral, Cher comes back. She comes back into my class instead of the class above, and she has that stupid hat, black and padded, to protect her head.

"Hi," says Cher, coming to sit next to me. Her face is empty.

"Hi," I say, moving up a bit to give her space. We don't smile. It's like new people meeting.

"Iola," says Ms Thomas, "Show Cher where we're up to."

So I take the book she's given Cher, the one we're all reading together, and I find her the page. Twenty-three. And Cher says "Thank you," slowly and then Ms Thomas keeps right on reading as if nothing is different.

The girls keep turning round to look at Cher in her stupid hat and, turning back, they laugh into their hands. Cher doesn't notice. She's pretending to read. I watch her. Her finger moves across the page but her eyes don't follow it. She's goes on like that right the way until lunchtime. When the bell goes, I don't wait for her to speak to me, I just leave the class straight away.

I'm sitting on my step, scratching with my stone on the concrete slab when Cher plonks herself down next to me. My whole body turns into concrete. She'll ask me. She'll ask me about Pigeon. Her dad.

But she doesn't. She just says, "Hi," and nothing else. And then she sits there. Staring straight ahead. Efa's right. Cher's not the same since the accident.

All we say is "Hi", most days. She doesn't speak much. And since then, this is the way we've been. One month after the other, until the summer, and the one month after the other all through the year. Time passes. Time passes by like watching fields through the window of a train.

21

"You're a big reader aren't you, lad?" Allan says to Pigeon.

Pigeon just stares at him and says nothing. Allan looks at him in *that* way. But Pigeon doesn't care; he just puts his book under his arm and walks out of Education Block into the centre.

"What d'you get?" asks Neil as he goes past Pigeon, "Fairytale?"

Pigeon ignores him, keeps on walking along the corridor to his room.

In their room Salim's asleep as usual. Pigeon lies on his bed and opens the book. There's a lot of pictures of space that look like photographs but aren't. They're done with a computer. They're pretty, the pictures of space. There are super nova and nebulae, and the most awesome thing about them is that they're far away. Pigeon likes that word, 'awesome'. Not the way the kids here use it, not with an exclamation mark after it. 'Awesome!' No. But 'awesome', said quietly and full of fear. Big and almost frightening, but beautiful. Awesome. Like the nebulae in this book. So far away that you can't even imagine it, the distance, and so big that you're not important at all. In the books about space you can find so many things which you couldn't see or understand with your own eyes and mind.

Pigeon turns the pages, and it's as if there isn't the centre all around him, as if he isn't somewhere between concrete and walls and roofing, not hours away from the hill, and his town, not in England. It's as if the sky is open above him and full to the brim with stars, with shimmering lights, galaxies that whir like cogs, and super nova which burst full of every colour he can imagine.

When he wakes his face is against the sleek page of the book. There's the sound of the bell, the sound that's for lessons and learning and seeing the others.

"Salim," says Pigeon. "Wake up."

Salim groans and turns over too. Salim's older than Pigeon is, and bigger. But he's gentle and quiet, and he doesn't mind that Pigeon doesn't much like to talk. He's given up on that, Pigeon, given up on lining up the words and setting them in patterns that make sense. It's a lie. And anyway, if he were to talk here, for real, no one would understand. Salim's the same. Pigeon's heard him, on the phone, talking to his mam. They speak in an up and down and fast way. It's Urdu, Salim says. Urdu. So maybe Salim feels like Pigeon. Like his mouth's been shut up same as his body has.

"Hey Taffy!" Big Neil calls after Pigeon as Pigeon and Salim are walking towards Education Block. It's because he's Welsh, although Pigeon's never heard the word before, Taffy, and he doesn't feel anything. He doesn't feel Welsh. He's just Pigeon, just Pigeon.

It's important here, where you're from. It's funny how it's so important, considering everyone here lives the same life, eats the same food, gets up at the same time, and has lights out just at the same moment.

"Fucking Taffy," says Big Neil again as they're going into Education Block "I heard your lot're all related. Mum and dad brother and sister are they? You can tell by the look on you. Ugh. And that language's so ugly it makes me want to puke. Say that sound again. The one that sounds like you're going to be sick."

Pigeon looks at Neil, and says it: "CH".

"Say a word with it in."

"Cachwr," says Pigeon.

"What's that mean?"

"Arsehole," says Pigeon bracing for the kick that lands in his gut.

Salim's pulled Neil off him within seconds, and the warden's squaring up, wading in.

"Alright S," says Neil to Salim backing off. "Keep your knickers on."

It's good having Salim on side.

Pigeon nods to the warden that it's alright and the warden backs off. He doesn't want trouble either.

They go through to where Allan's stood waiting. You go in and the closer to the back of the room you are, the harder you are. Where Pigeon and Salim sit, near the front, the desk has been scratched full of names. So many names that Pigeon can't read them. What's the point in the letters? The desk is just noise.

Neil barges past Pigeon and wipes something sticky on his face as he goes. It's the oil they put on the hinges of the doors here, black and dirty; it always gets on your hands. Pigeon wipes it off his cheek. He looks down at the names, the other names, of all the kids who've sat at this desk. All the kids who were too soft, like him, to sit at the back. Danny. Mark. And there it is, the name Pigeon likes to look at. Neil.

Still, Pigeon's looking forward to this. Geography. Geography is massive forces and being part of a bigger picture.

But Neil talks all the way through at the back of the class so he can't listen or think. Sometimes Neil throws things at Pigeon, even when the teacher's watching. A rubber, a pencil, an old piece of chewed gum.

"Neil," says Allan. And then "Neil," again.

Pigeon doesn't care. Allan gives them all a worksheet, and on the worksheet there are the tectonic plates moving back and forth and making whole countries afraid. At the end of the class Allan asks for the worksheets back. Pigeon carefully folds his under the table, to take back to his room. The stories have stopped, what's got Pigeon interested now is FACTS.

Take the first FACT. That Iola killed Him. Even that takes some working out. Did she or didn't she? Wasn't it Pigeon got the gun, and wasn't it Pigeon anyway who made it happen? And isn't it Pigeon that is proud and happy about it, and she that's carrying on with her life? There's a difference between facts and what is real isn't there? Which is why he can't imagine some of the things in the space books. All that isn't real for him. You can't really know those facts. You can't really know that space is curved, or that the light you see in the sky when this star shines has disappeared: the star is really gone and the light is thousands of years old. It *was* thousands of years old. The star isn't. It *was*. It's like saying that she'd done it. You can't prove it with your own eyes and ears, so does it matter? Somewhere he still knows it. She'd done it, not him. But looking at his life, it makes sense if it was Pigeon pulling the catch away on the gun and getting ready to fire it. Enough people think it for it just to be that way. And anyway, hasn't he finally changed things? It wasn't her. It was him. It was him, and so everything here is worth it. You need to get the facts straight, so you can know what to do.

Pigeon tries to think what to do, sitting in his room with Salim, the centre around them and a fence around that. He tries to think. But however he thinks about it it doesn't make any difference to the fact that Big Neil, Salim and all of the others are stuck here together. All of them closed up in the Centre together. Crammed in like too many teeth in a shut mouth.

22

If I close the door I can put the radio on loud and Efa won't hear, or, she might hear but she won't complain and shout up the stairs about the music she calls rubbish and trash and all that. It's Atlantic 252 and Wet Wet Wet, again, and I'm swaying round the room thinking of Llion, and last night.

Llion, with his black hair and his white skin, kissed me round the back of the wall after the disco. He'd not danced with me for the slow dances, but it was after, when we were all out on the street and fooling around laughing and joking and some of the boys with cans of beer and some of them smoking. It was then he gave me the signal. He did it with his head, motioning it from one side to the other, a kind of nod towards the wall. Then you had to go behind the wall and kiss him, and his tongue was wet like an eel, but his lips were soft and it was good to be close to him. His hands were up my skirt, and I didn't stop him until he was inside my knickers. His hands were dry and fidgety.

"Stopia wan," I said then, and I laughed, and for a few seconds he didn't stop and then he did.

The music on the radio swells again, all full of love and happy endings and I sway in the room with that feeling of spring coming. Perhaps Llion will ask me out properly now I've kissed him. Or perhaps he won't. The music changes on the radio, and it's a rap song, American, angry and about love. To this song I think about how I'll feel if he doesn't ask me out. Angry, and sad at the same time. Rejected. It's a sore feeling, but almost delicious too, and you know you'll have to come back to it, like picking a scab.

I know Cher's coming up the stairs before Efa shouts to tell me. I hear the familiar thump of Cher's slow, heavy feet. Then Efa calls.

"Iola. Cher's coming up! Efa's voice is thin and bare, like an old, frayed guitar string. I can always hear Cher coming up the stairs anyway, Efa doesn't need to announce it, but I'm glad she has, Efa, because it's speaking to each other, and we don't do much of that now, and Efa'd said my name. *Iola*. And that's speaking to me. Directly.

Cher knocks on the door of my bedroom. You always have to knock. Everyone needs 'privacy'.

When I open the door Cher's stood in the doorway, panting from coming up the stairs, from carrying her own body, which is awkward and big. Cher's stood there, with the same slow expression she always has ever since *then*.

"Come in. Listen!" I tell her.

The song that's on the radio's full of drums and a high voice that's like a computer, it's good and it makes your heart thump to hear it.

Cher listens without moving for a bit. She's like a dog now sometimes, Cher. Does what she's told.

"Yes," she says, "that's good that is," and stands listening until the song peters into a man and a woman talking and telling jokes on the radio. I turn them down.

"What happened to you last night anyway?" I ask. I hadn't seen Cher after going round the wall with Llion. I'd had to walk back by myself, up the path from town, and it'd been sad and lonely and dark, so I couldn't help thinking about things.

Cher frowns.

"I saw you with Llion, so I went." Cher's voice is flat. She's jealous. You can tell she's jealous.

I laugh a bit. Perhaps Cher will ask me now, about Llion? But she doesn't. Cher doesn't. It's like it's nothing, what happened with Llion. Like it doesn't mean anything. But this feeling, of Llion in those few moments when he didn't stop, even when I'd asked him to. And it was uncomfortable. And what if it didn't mean anything?

Meaningless. The big empty word comes into my head. Meaningless.

Cher and me head out to go downtown to try on clothes. As we walk down we have to go past Cher's house, Pigeon's house, where there's still his mam inside. Whenever I look into the house there's his mam, still sewing, and around the window are all the dresses she's made, hanging. It's always dark in the house, and it's like an old memory. I never go in anymore. Pigeon's shed's like a crumpled photograph, fading there in the garden, and when you look through the windows, you can see nothing's moved and there's still one of Pigeon's magazines open at the page he was reading before he went. The magazine's covered in dust. Cher says Pigeon's mam doesn't like her moving anything.

Today I don't look, but I know she's inside. I see Cher throw a nervous glance towards her as we pass the house, but I know not to say anything. We had that conversation, a few weeks ago, and it didn't go so well.

We'd been sitting on the wall by the park. I was scratching my name into the wall with a stone. Cher was just sitting.

"Pigeon's mam said you were there," Cher'd said. "She said she saw you outside, you were there when it happened."

Pigeon's mam's called Mari Davies, but no one calls her that. 'Mari' sounds like she must've been part of the town once, and she never was. Pigeon's mam, Mari Davies, was someone people had to ignore. It was a shame, people said, about Mari Davies.

"No, I wasn't."

I felt cross, I kept scratching with the stone. I was on the O. The I had gone slightly skewed, off to one side, in italics, as if it was a pretend I, not one I really meant.

"She says you were." Cher turned to face me.

"She's confused. His mam's just confused."

Cher starts walking again. Two steps or three, and then.

"Why would she say it, if it wasn't true?"

"I dunno, Cher. She's crazy."

"I dunno," says Cher, looking at me funny. Cher and Pigeon's mam are close. Cher talks about her all the time. It was Pigeon's mam who got Cher better. Going to see her every day. It's as if she's Cher's mam, not Pigeon's.

"What're you saying?" I snap. I can feel my whole body buzzing, and that sound in my ears, that killing sound.

I started to cry and that ended it. I started to cry and then I pushed Cher over, toppled the big body onto the tarmac. I turned at the corner, and Cher was still sitting there, looking down at herself in her pink dress. She'd never been the same, Cher, since the accident. That's what everyone says here "Di 'rioed 'di bod cystal. Rioed 'di bod 'run un." They shake their heads as they say it. Shake their heads.

After that conversation, Cher stayed off the subject. But whenever I walk past Pigeon's house it's there. It's all there, and you can't ignore it. It's like an itch inside your head, and around your ribs there's that feeling again, even all these days past, and almost years, there's still a feeling, like a held breath, like the chicken meat Dad used to package at the factory, all held in and without air.

It'll go. It's a feeling that will go one day, like bad weather always does. It'll go. Because when you do something bad and you're a kid, the punishment doesn't last. And anyway, it was Pigeon.

I've got that straight now. It was Pigeon. He'd done it. And that *is* true. Because he'd got it all set up and got the gun and it was his anger that'd done it, nothing much to do with me. And that's why my life's got to go on, and his has to stop for now. Because he'd done it. Everything except kill Him.

But that's such a heavy thing to carry with me past his house, and past his mam who's alone and crazy these days in that house. It's heavy. However much I think it, that it's him, this heavy feeling's mine and I'm on my own with it.

23

It was all worth it, because he felt so proud. Perhaps it was even worth it when later on that day Salim was out speaking to his mother on the phone, and Neil came into the room, into the open cell Pigeon and Salim shared, walking in like he owned it, with two other lads behind him. They jumped on Pigeon, and when their hitting was like a storm and their fists like water boiling and beating in his ears and against his shoulders, his back, his ribs, perhaps even then it was worth it? Because at least he'd got Him.

But here it was almost like it had been at home, or worse, because when you shouted then, for someone to come, for Mam, for Iola, at least someone might hear, and understand. Here there was nobody. The words that were him, were Pigeon, were useless. His words made sounds and shapes that nobody could see. Nobody heard. Nobody listened.

You could see it in the wardens' eyes when they turned away from Pigeon: It was better to let the kids get a handle on him, that one. He needed to be knocked into shape. Besides, the lads never did any lasting damage. Knew when to stop.

Because of Allan asking, they did take him to see a psychologist. *Are you alright Pigeon?* Is everything alright. But you couldn't think of the right words for all this, not in English, so you couldn't speak, it was like having a mouth full of dry bread. You couldn't speak.

Did he understand that his mother was ill? That word 'de-te-rio-ra-tion'. Did he understand? Did he know what he'd done? Did he understand the terms that they'd used at the trial? Self-defence, unpremeditated, psychological trauma. These were all words used to describe Pigeon and what he'd done.

Yes he understood them. He learnt some of those words. Pigeon could give you a definition if you wanted. Res-pon-si-bi-li-ty he knew. Knew the answer to did he feel responsible? Yes. Did he regret it? Yes. But that was a lie.

And then came the other questions. What did he want to do when he was older? He wanted to build walls. Walls? Yes. Stone ones? Yes. Tall, straight stone walls. He wanted to build walls between things. Things? Places. People. He could tell you that. He could tell you in words that didn't get close to the inside of him, not close to the shed, the crooked house, the hill, and not close to telling you about the fists and the door that closed each night and left the room smothered and dangerous.

It was because you couldn't get the measure of him, Pigeon. He wasn't speaking to you directly. You couldn't trust him. There was something not right. "There's something wrong with you," they'd whisper in his ear. And he knew it. Knew it was because of the words that were inside, stopping him up. Stopping him from talking the talk that you needed here. He worked hard at it, putting his own words out, one by one, until the whispers stopped, and the quick, fluent English comebacks and threats fell from his mouth too, as if he was one of them.

Visting times were the best. Salim's mother came to see him every weekday so Pigeon had the room to himself. His mam never came. It was too far, and difficult for her on the bus. He sent her letters still and now his caseworker'd got in touch with her. She was doing better. She was doing better now they said. That was good. Perhaps she'd be able to hear him and speak to him when he came home.

One time Salim took Pigeon with him to see his mother. They walked into the visiting area. Pigeon had never been there before. It was all chairs and tables, and people in little groups, sitting. Pigeon could see Neil there, talking to a man with hair full of gel. Neil had a real life too. Pigeon felt glad about it. Neil had a real life too. All this was just a bit of it. Tem-po-ra-ry, he thought.

"This way," said Salim. "That's her over there."

Salim's mum was dressed in clothes like an Arab woman on the telly. She stood up and smiled at Salim. She kissed his cheeks like a mother would. She spoke to him like a mother in quick bubbling Urdu.

"Mum, this is my friend, Pigeon," said Salim, shyly.

Pigeon didn't know what to do. He wanted her to like him. He extended a hand. That was what you did when you were grown up wasn't it?

She stepped towards him, and she kissed him on the cheek just like she had with Salim. Her face was soft and kind, and as she kissed him she held his shoulders.

"Thank you," she said smiling, with eyes like summer "Thank you for being a friend to Salim."

Pigeon could feel himself starting to cry. He could feel the shaking travelling up from his feet to his hips and up his back. He couldn't do it.

Pigeon ran out.

"Pigeon!" he could hear Salim shouting after him. The wardens stepped aside to let him pass. Pigeon ran back to the room, and threw himself on the bed. He bit his own hand to stop the tears. They couldn't see him cry. They couldn't.

After that Pigeon decided visiting times were the best, because he could read the books and be alone in the room. But he'd finished the space book now. He closed it, closed up the open sky.

They offered him a visit home.

"You could go home for a weekend," the woman said. The psychologist.

"Why?" he asked.

"To see your mum."

"She doesn't care," he said.

"It's not that she doesn't care," said this woman who knew nothing about anything "She's just been ill."

Ill? Was that what they called it when you just let yourself disappear. Was he supposed to treat his mother like she was his patient, or his child? Was that what they wanted?

"No thanks," he said. "I'll just stick around here."

Allan, in Education, had got it into his head that he could help Pigeon. That made it worse. That Allen thought reading and writing help would do it, make Pigeon's problems go away.

"We need to get your English going," he said to Salim and Pigeon. "I want you to leave here speaking and writing it like pros."

Salim looked blank, and Pigeon scowled. It was just another way of saying he wasn't right. On the hill language had been something he had. He'd got smart with it. Twisting it. Turning it. So that it said what you wanted it to, and so other people believed what you said. Here all that was lost. Just a ghost. An accent when Pigeon spoke English. An imperfection.

Pigeon pretended he couldn't read Allan's English words until Allan almost gave up, stumped by Pigeon's slow, painful reading.

"C'mon, lad," he said once, looking at Pigeon. "You can do better than that."

I can in Welsh, was what Pigeon thought. I can in my own fucking language.

But slowly Pigeon learnt that English was a weapon, and could be a shield. You needed it in pristine condition, and you needed the tricks of it, so you could defend yourself. Your own language was a part of your body, like a shoulder or a thigh, and when you were hurt there was no defence. When the kids argued in Welsh at home on the hill it was a bare knuckled fight. But English. With English what you had to do was build armour, and stand there behind your shield to shoot people down. Pigeon buried his own language deeper and deeper in that armour. Until the beatings stopped.

Salim wasn't able. They came for him. Time after time. Until one day Salim was taken off the wing. Pigeon never knew what happened to him. He was sent home, the lads said. But where was home for Salim? You never really knew.

Then it was the long last months alone, with only the quiet pale boy called John for company. And he wasn't Salim. John was serious and pale, and thin and disappearing. Pigeon buried missing Salim under as many new English words as he could. Now, in education. Pigeon sat at the back of the class. John sat at the front. So you had to not speak to John. You had to let him learn.

Pigeon was somebody now. When he walked down the corridors, people shrank away. It was all just reputation. Pigeon spread stories about himself. He was tough, he was strong. He'd killed a grown man. And, as usual, you never quite knew if all of it was true.

Allan kept hoping for Pigeon. And, secretly, Pigeon kept learning, sneaking books around, under his clothes, under his bedclothes, raiding them for worlds where none of this was happening.

Allan kept quiet about it.

"Enjoy it?" he'd whisper when Pigeon brought a book back, watching him pull it shiftily from under his jumper, checking with nervous eyes to see if any of the others had seen.

"Nah," Pigeon'd say. But he'd grin. And Allan'd grin too. He was alright that kid, Pigeon. Whatever the others said, that kid was alright.

It was Allan who told him.

"You're due out next month," he said, looking Pigeon straight in the eye.

Pigeon said nothing. He took a step back. Impossible. It felt impossible. Most of the lads here knew when they were due, but he'd forgotten. There was no one to tell him. No visitors to keep him thinking about Home.

"We need to make a plan for it," said Allan "Get you set up with a plan so it goes well for you back home."

But Pigeon just stared at Allan. He was due out. Pigeon felt small, grey, nondescript. He felt terrified, his mouth full of too much stifling quietness.

According to Allan, it was to be home and then just keeping up with lessons and everything and 'staying out of trouble'. What did that mean? Trouble was the house, was the hill, was his mam, was Iola, was everything he had inside his head and everything that was making its way slowly, day by day, to the tip of his tongue.

24

Walking downtown, we both ignore the crooked house as we pass it. Cher goes on about the exams.

"Iola," she asks me slowly, "did you study yet?"

Cher's English is like a slow song. It goes up and down, and some of the letters are pulled out long. She never learnt Welsh after all, Cher, only a few words and they sound out of tune in her mouth. Before the accident Cher'd been learning it automatically, like all the kids who move here do, but after the accident, the words just didn't stick.

Cher means for the exams, have I started revising?

"Nah," I say. But Cher gives me a slow, sly look that means don't believe you.

It's been all paper and pens and writing and thinking about school ever since Pigeon left. All hard work, that's what it's been, all through one school year, and then into another, and up to secondary. That's because they think you must be good if your marks are. My marks are top or second top. You can keep safe in good marks. I keep my grades high.

Cher doesn't. Her writing was like a kid's when she first came back. I'd got set a task of helping her with reading. We didn't do much reading but Cher is cleverer and funnier than you'd think once you give her time, and so we're friends now. Until the last couple of months the other girls weren't much interested in me anyway, because I don't do sport or have nice clothes and until last year I was short. This year I've grown and got those new trousers and I'm getting some looks from the boys now, you can see it. They've got interested, the boys. Interested enough for behind the wall anyway. So now the girls are paying attention at school too, and it'll be a dangerous time. A dangerous time of back and forth looks, and words that scar you across the back along the school corridors and up the town's darkening streets where the air is turning black with the tit for tat insults of the girls. The girls are all like that. We're all like that. Becoming a woman is so embarrassing. You feel it. The shame. And so you've got to lash out.

But there's none of that with Cher. That's the thing about Cher. Since the accident you can depend on her. She's regular. There's nothing lively uncoiling in her with that dangerous electricity that fills the bodies of all the other girls. *Womanliness.* Efa calls it. Womanliness. A warm word.

Still, I feel cold when we pass Pigeon's house. I feel it again, the feeling of that day.

Walking downtown, we're almost at the shop. You don't want anyone to see you going in, because it's a charity shop. It'd be "Iola Williams wears dead people's clothes", it'd be "sloppy seconds Iola" and all that. So me and Cher walk along the High Street, past Nasareth Chapel which is closed now and boarded up, and has a sign that says For Sale. They say someone'll buy it and make it into flats, even though you can't imagine it. How can they make that chapel into somewhere for someone to live? That should've lasted forever, even if we didn't go. It was just a place that existed and should always exist. But it's over. The chapel's over. It's like a big dead person lying on a slab.

Then there's Spar, the Chemists, and then the British Heart Foundation shop.

We look quickly up and down the street. There's no one we know, it's too early for kids to be sitting on the bench on the street. A good time. We go in quickly.

Inside the shop there's clothes and Luned behind the counter. We ask Luned if we can try on some of the clothes. She's old as chapel, Luned, grey hair and skin like a windy sea. But she still works here every Saturday, and she doesn't mind Cher and me trying things on even though we won't buy anything.

"Gewch siwr," she says nodding and smiling. "Gewch siwr."

She smiles at me, but looks at Cher a bit differently. They do that. It's since the accident, and because of her way of speaking slowly and staring at people. Now when she does it, I'll kick her or nudge her and she'll say "Sorry" and laugh.

You have to look and look along all the rails. Mostly it's things you'll never wear, or things that are too big. But you might find something decent if you have a good look around. Today it's all just trying things on. We don't have any money anyway. I find a skirt for Cher. Cher still has good legs, at the bottom, below the knee. Above the knee they're too fat. Having a perfect body means having all the details right. The shape of you going out and in at all the right places, all your skin smooth, all the dips and curves just perfect. Cher grins when she sees the skirt. It's going to be the right size. It'll look good. You never get to see Cher looking as good as when she tries on clothes in the shop; she only wears big jumpers and old scraggy leggings, and pumps. And her hair's a mess, and she never puts it up except in one long ponytail that looks just like a pony's greasy tail. Cher picks out a body top and some trousers for me. They're OK, and it's the rules that we have to try on what the other one chooses, even if it's gross.

We go into the changing room together. We've been doing this every Saturday for ages, but for the last few times it's felt different. My body's got more shape now, WOMANLY, and my boobs are heavier, and next to me, stood in the mirror Cher looks fat and is still the shape of a girl. I quickly put the body top on, and the trousers, and then realise Cher's just staring.

"What?" I ask her.

"Sorry," says Cher. "Sorry."

But I don't feel right in the changing room with Cher, and it might be the last time we do it because there was something not right in the way Cher was staring. There was something not right. Cher doesn't ask me what I think of the skirt, Cher hardly looks at herself in the mirror and then she takes the skirt off, puts the leggings back on, and gets out quick.

A few weeks later, Cher and me are sitting on the sofa.

"Efa's got a boyfriend," I tell her. I can't stop my voice sounding surprised. I can't help my voice sounding like Efa had no right. And anyway how had she found the time between The Home and all that?

"Iola," Efa'd said that morning. "Tyrd. Come and sit here, Iola."

I thought then, for a minute, that she knew, Efa. This'd be it, I'd go over to sit at her side and then my Efa'd say it. I know what you did, Iola, she'd say. And how would it feel? Would it feel bad, or good. Perhaps it would. Perhaps it wouldn't be so heavy if she shared it.

But it wasn't that.

"Iola, I'm seeing someone."

"What? Who?"

"His name's Dafydd."

"Dafydd?"

"Yes."

I stare at my sister. A man? Efa? What about *It's a world unfair for women, love* and all that? What about Taid? What about Dad?

"I'll have him round soon," Efa said. "So you can meet him."

"She's been seeing that guy for ages," says Cher now, in her even way, starting slowly and then breathing along what she's going to say, so it comes out all together in a sort of slow singsong.

"How'd you know?"

There's a pause while Cher starts to speak, finds the words, like gathering over-ripe blackberries.

"I've seen them together."

"Where?"

"Downtown."

"When?"

"When I went to the shop," Cher pauses. "On my own," she adds

It'd been the day after she'd stared at me in the changing room in that way.

She hadn't asked me to go. It was between us, that long look she'd given my body and legs that day. It was stuck between us, and it wasn't going anywhere. Cher had bought that skirt there. That's how I knew she'd been. It was the first time either of us had spent a penny in Luned's shop.

Efa brings him round. He comes into the house and steps over the doorstep, and the light in the kitchen's different. The first day he comes, Efa makes curry. It's nice. I eat it, and listen to them talk.

"How long did it take you to train?" Efa's asking him.

Dafydd, it turns out, is a yoga teacher. He can do yoga better than Efa, according to her. His face is full of smiles. He looks healthy, like as if he's just been on holiday, all year. Dafydd has long fingers, they dance around like leaves. He has dark hair, and honey-coloured skin. It looks like the sunshine, his skin, not like rain.

They're sitting on the sofa, talking, ignoring me.

"Oh, a couple of years. We've got a retreat coming up, Efa," he says. "Why don't you come?"

Efa jerks her head towards me. It's because of me she can't go.

"Could she stay with a friend?" he asks.

I look at Dafydd. He smiles. Efa looks at me, and then she looks at him. And maybe this is going to be like when He moved in with Pigeon? Maybe it'll be getting chucked out for me. But Dafydd smiles. Maybe not.

Cher comes and stays when Efa's away. Efa says that's alright.

"Ma'n well i ti gael cwmni," she says.

But being with Cher's almost like being on your own. I'm reading a magazine. Cher's leaning against the sink. The light comes in from the window behind Cher, green through the wet leaves outside and the window. You just get a bit of sunshine, like its shining through water.

"Have you seen the way she looks at him?" Cher says it almost angrily.

Cher doesn't like Dafydd. Cher says she's seen him smoking,

even though I can't imagine it. Cher scowled when she found out Dafydd had come round.

"I know," I say. Efa does go all stupid when Dafydd's there.

"I mean, he's horrible." Cher's not keen on men anyways.

"Leave it Cher, OK? Efa's happy. I'm happy."

"He's horrible," says Cher again.

"Why Cher? What's he done to you?"

Cher's just playing with the fridge door, opening and closing it with a sucky click. She's tall now, taller than me, but she's still wide.

"He's horrible. Just is."

Cher grabs a carton of juice from the fridge and goes out the door, leaving me and my magazine, and all these pretty girls in it with skin smooth like new paper. Cher's moving faster now, speaking quicker, and she's got more opinions. It doesn't feel so safe to be around her. She does things of her own accord.

But he's nice to me, Dafydd, really nice. And he hugs Efa and she laughs and acts like a little girl. Which is funny, to think of Efa being a little girl. I don't think Efa's ever been that before, not really. Not with The Home and all that.

But Cher still doesn't like Dafydd. And the feeling's mutual. Dafydd, when he arrives with his car full of boxes, looks down, smiling at Cher, and says "Haia Cher," like as if he's just pretending to say the name, like it's stupid. He knows her. How does he know her?

Cher and Dafydd don't get on. Cher almost never talks to him. When they're both around, which they are most of the time, Cher looks angry. She gets a black look and her eyelids are like dark hoods over her eyes. Efa says she's jealous, "Cos we've a man in our house now, and Cher doesn't have a Dad."

"I don't have a Dad either," I tell Cher. "He upped and left, and I'm not interested." But it doesn't make a difference, and Cher just looks confused.

And I don't know quite why I do it, but I make Cher angry, giving Dafydd all the attention, and stroking his head and hugging him while Cher scowls on the sofa. Dafydd grabs me then, and pulls me onto his knee, as if I'm still a little kid, and he teases me about my clothes, which are too small now because I've grown. Efa smiles, and then me and Efa laugh like we used to back in the day. But Cher ruins it. Cher storms out with Efa going after her saying "Cher?" out the door. It's not until Efa and Cher are gone that I get up, cos being on Dafydd's knee without Cher and Efa feels strange.

I follow on after Cher then, passing Efa on the street who's turning back to go to Dafydd on the sofa. When I catch up with Cher and grab her arm, Cher whirls round.

"Piss off, Iola," she says. And it's then I see she's crying. And I feel bad. I didn't mean to. I didn't mean to.

"Sorry," I say, but it sounds too quick. And I am sorry, but I'm not quite sure what for. Which part.

I'm still stood there, holding Cher's arm, and then Cher does it. She leans forwards and she kisses me, on the lips. Cher's lips are clean and soft.

I pull away, like I've touched something hot. And me and Cher stand facing. We stand a long while.

"Lets go down to the river, Cher," I say then.

"Alright," says Cher. And that's it. Nothing's broken. She follows me down the hill, like a stray.

"Will Pigeon be back soon?"

We've sat down now together, my head's on Cher's lap and Cher's stroking my hair, Cher's other hand's curling round my belly when she says it suddenly. It's a good thing Pigeon's gone, so Cher can be friends with me, and we can sit and cuddle and touch while we lean against the big tree by the river.

But Cher keeps asking, "Will he be back soon?"

"No," I say. I'm cross with Cher again, and push her off.

Cher won't let it go. She wants to know about Pigeon's trial. All about Pigeon, like as if I could really tell her Pigeon's story, or like I really know anything except for that I miss him, and that without him nothing ever happens, and nothing ever matters, like Cher.

"Lets go and see him," says Cher then. "Lets go and see him."

"No," I say, and I stand up.

"Why?" asks Cher, and her eyes are big and brown and soft, like feathers and cushions and cotton wool.

"We don't know where he is."

"He's in Liverpool," says Cher.

I stop. *In England?* Pigeon?

"How d'you know?"

"I saw it on a letter. They wrote and said we could visit."

"Well you can't."

"Why not?"

"Cher! He killed your dad!"

I say it. And it's then it hurts me. The feeling like panic up my body and in my chest. I can't breathe. What's wrong? What's wrong with me? I can hear sounds in my head, can hear people shouting in my head. It's all terrible, big, dark. And then I'm just stood here on the grass again with Cher. Cher's watching me. She just watches me and watches me until I go back to normal. Cher picks up a stone, and plays with it in her hand.

"So?" she says.

"What do you mean, so?"

"He was a bastard," she says then. And then she laughs. Cher laughs.

Under the curls, there's a spot on Cher's forehead I just want to squeeze.

"He's gone anyways, Iola," she says. And her voice is kind. As if she understands. And it feels like some of that pressure lifts, just like a tiny bit of a breeze on a heavy day.

But there's no way of getting rid of him, Pigeon. Not for good. He'll be back. And there's part of me can't wait, and part of me that'd rather wait forever.

25

In the lit-up window, bright against the houses and the hill, there's the girl. Bare except for her underwear, she stands in her room beside the bed. A selection of clothing lies across the bedcover. She places each trouser and shoe combination together, stands back, considers. Pacing over to the radio, she turns 'Atlantic 252' up a notch. Through the window it blares, Wet Wet Wet *again*.

Skipping back to the clothes, she holds the tops up against herself in the mirror, puts her head to one side, smiles at herself, then adjusts her lips so that her teeth don't show so much. Half the decision made, she picks up a little make-up compact, kneels on the floor at the foot of the tall mirror and lifts the eyeliner to the rim of her eye, to carefully, shakily, trace all around it. She layers her lashes with black mascara. She lifts the pad of the eye-shadow and dabs it over her eyelid. A love song comes on the radio and she begins to sway dreamily.

Make-up assembled, she stands up again, still in full view of the window, the faint trace of her ribs showing above her fragile waist, a small bra covering her almost breasts. She pulls the body-top over her, buttons it at the crotch, and stands to survey.

She does a pirouette, one leg bending as she spins and the tip of its toe finding the hollow in the side of the other knee.

In the overgrown garden, stood between the old, ivied sculptures, a big bag slung over one shoulder, Pigeon watches the dark house. He almost laughs, and watches again, eyes held by the spotlighted room as Iola pulls on her jeans and stands critically, looking at herself in the mirror.

There's the sound of feet on the gravel, and, through the darkness Pigeon peers, to see someone else there, in the garden, watching. He's stood behind the tree. A man. Tall, strong-looking shoulders. The man's too old to be watching Iola. Much too old. Pigeon goes up behind him.

"Hey!" he says, and when the guy turns round, Pigeon kicks him in the balls.

The man doubles over, and Pigeon scarpers off out the garden and down the street. He runs uphill. Uphill to the crooked house.

The man doesn't follow, so, Pigeon, sprinting up the dark street, begins to slow down. He slows, stops, turns. It's just an empty street, streetlights, bins, a navy-black sky, quiet, only the sound of a faint television coming from one of the houses and an uneasy breeze brushing over it all.

Pigeon walks up this street, turns, left, right, walks a downhill street and now, it's his lane, and now his door. Pigeon reaches the door. Stands.

His mam had made it in for the exit interview. She'd sat there silently while Pigeon answered all their questions. They decided that although she seemed to be not quite all there. It'd do. He was old enough to manage anyway. Pigeon couldn't bear to look at her, but he caught the faint smell of the crooked house from her clothes.

On leaving day, today, she was supposed to come and collect him. They weren't supposed to sign him out otherwise. But the social worker had called. His mam was unwell again. She couldn't come. They shouldn't send him home to her without her signing. But they did. Pigeon was going to be old enough soon anyway, and he persuaded them, persuaded them with his tight, smooth English, so they did.

Leaving the centre, he'd felt the world slowly fix back together, but the joins between things were uneven, piecemeal, and now, standing here on the doorstep, the world has collapsed again. There's only a blur and Pigeon and the door. The door is made of PVC now. There's double-glazing. There's a knocker. But Pigeon raises his fist to the door. He hesitates.

When he knocks, he can feel the street shattering behind him. His body is warm against the cool street. His mam may make him arrive. That's possible. Pigeon waits on the doorstep for her. He musn't breathe.

When she opens he looks at her full in the face for the first time. She's still beautiful. And she's still not back to normal. She looks at him, in silence.

It's a long while.

"Pigeon," she says eventually. And she smiles, she smiles so softly, like slow-dappling sunshine. And it's so innocent her smile. It's so innocent. And Pigeon knows as always that she's not to blame. She isn't to blame for any of it.

"O nghariad i," she says, "Oh my love, my love."

And now it's her words that get lost on the way to his ears, because Pigeon can't answer. Pigeon says nothing, steps past his mother into the house.

The living room is dark, and dusty. Pigeon goes in, and opens the curtains. The moon makes tracings of familiar furniture. He turns on the light. The old bulb flickers briefly, and then dies. In its few moments of brightness, the room's dirty. There's dust all over everything.

"Mum!" he says in English "You can't bloody live like this."

He walks straight through to the kitchen, grabs the bin, and brings it back to the living room, starts pushing all the old cans and bottles that litter the floor into it. He even picks up one of Efa's dust-covered magazine without recognition and thrusts it into the bin.

His mam stares at him. She stands, holding the edge of the chair and stares.

Pigeon doesn't stop clearing until there's some kind of order. He finds a bulb for the light, screws it in. Switches it on. He decides the curtains just need to be pulled down. They're so faded and moth-eaten. They go into the bin too. Pigeon starts beating out the sofa cushions, filling the room with the dust of all these stagnant days in the house. Pigeon opens the windows. Cold air rushes in, blows away memory. Blows away the shape of Him, lying here, on the floor, blood running from his head. Pigeon rips up the carpet, takes that outside too. Then he brushes the hard quarry-tiled floor. Brushes and brushes it, under his mother's gaze, and mops it too. There's only washing up liquid to use for the mopping, but it still cleans it all away. His mam stands holding the edge of the chair until he's finished. He cleans around her feet, not asking her to move.

"There you are, Mam," he says when he's done, "You can sit down now."

She sits down, slowly, hesitantly. Looks up at him, and the light that grows slowly, weakly across her face might be a smile.

Next Pigeon goes upstairs. One room for his Mam, one for him. He takes a bin liner with him, and starts tipping into it anything that belonged to Him or to Cher. He fills two bin liners within a few minutes. He strips the beds. Carries the sheets down to the kitchen ready to wash, walking through the living room on his way.

"Hello."

The shape is a girl. She stands in the middle of the lit-up, stripped living room. She's a little shorter than Pigeon, but far wider than he is. She's wearing a pink dress. It hangs over her stomach.

Pigeon stops, stands still in the room. He wasn't expecting there to be anyone else. Just him. Just his mam.

"Pigeon!" says the girl.

She knows him. He looks at this girl's thick face. He looks at her. She's familiar. He knows her. He knows her well.

Pigeon sits down, staring at the girl. It's *her?*

"What're you doing here?" his voice is like a wall as he asks the question. His mam has sat back down, and is sewing, as if nothing has happened, not Liverpool, not that place, not Salim, or Neil, or any of it.

"Writing," says Cher, slowly. Her voice is unlike a real voice. She's like the old Cher seen through glasses that are too strong, and she sounds as if she's underwater, as if her voice comes through air that's as thick as soup. "Writing," she says again, and she points at an exercise book, open on the table. The handwriting on the open pages of the book is big and ugly.

Pigeon looks at her.

"What happened to you?" he asks, looks her up and down. In there he's learnt to be cruel when he's afraid.

Cher shrugs. Her brows knot together. He's made her unhappy.

"I had an accident. It was in the fair. It was a road accident." Cher says what she knows, and he knows.

There's a silence.

"What are you doing here?" he asks her again. His voice is leaden and dangerous.

She shrugs. He's made her unhappy again. He can see the thought, passing across her broad face: *why should I not be here?* It's a simple thought. Stupid.

This is his house. This is his house.

Pigeon sits down, and as he sits, the house moves around him, as if it's standing in an untenable posture. Cher sits down too. She's quiet. She knows the drill. There should be no words. No sudden movements. No thoughts or opinions other than his own. There's only him, Pigeon, his chair, his white hands, the cigarette he lights now, and around him, the house.

But Pigeon is different to Him. Pigeon's crying now. They sit, the three of them. Pigeon crying. His mam gently puts a hand on his shoulder, and Cher watches him. This boy that killed her father. This boy that finally killed Him.

"It wasn't me, Mam," he says.

"What, love?"

"It wasn't me killed him," again. Do the words even work?

"Oh, Pigeon," is all she says. And he can tell she thinks he's sick. Thinks he doesn't know himself. Doesn't know what he did and didn't do.

"It was Iola, Mam. She came in and she did it."

His mam says nothing. But when he looks up at Cher, she's smiling.

"I'll make us some dinner," she says. "I'll make us some beans."

26

When Efa answers the door, I'm sat on the sofa opposite. I've been reading a book. I'm halfway through the world of the book. There's a girl in it, and when she's hurt, you ache. I look up from the page when I hear the neat little knocks. Six.

Him.

"O," says Efa when she opens the door and sees him standing there. Efa turns to me. But I'm just sat here, looking at the doorway with him caught in it, like a framed picture.

It's a dark night in late April outside. This Pigeon, standing on *my* doorstep is different and the same. His different and similar face is white against the wet night air. Efa looks from me to Pigeon, from Pigeon to me. None of us say anything for a few seconds.

He's not a boy. Not anymore. He's something that's got out of a box, out of where he belongs. Pigeon and me catch eyes in the air. We share something in that look that makes me cold, then he makes a blank face again, for Efa.

"Hi," he says, in English.

"Pigeon?" says Efa. As if she even needs to ask. His is a face you would recognise, and even if he didn't still look so much like that boy, you'd know it was him from the smile.

He grins. "Yep," he says.

Efa starts to question him now.

"Pryd ddes ti'n ôl? Sut wyt ti? Sut ma' dy fam?" but his answers are short and in English.

"Friday. I'm fine. Mam's OK."

He looks over at me.

"How's it going?" he asks me.

I shrug. How can I answer that. How do I even talk to him?

But Efa invites him in. He comes in, sits down next to me. The sofa flinches. Efa goes through to the kitchen, starts on the phone to Dafydd. She really doesn't care. Pigeon sits next to me, making the sofa heavy, weighing down my whole house.

"I brought you something," says Pigeon, looking at me, looking right at me. He starts rustling in his pockets for it. He brings it out, offering it to me with his strange, familiar hands. It's wrapped in brown paper. He gives it to me. Looking at the paper, looking at this little parcel, I feel sick. But I begin to unwrap, my hands feeling like they belong to someone else.

It's just a magnifying glass, mottled and dusty.

"It's yours," he says quietly.

I stare at it. I stare at it, and in my head there's that statement, that statement:

Ma' Gwyn yn od.

It's an angry boy's voice, a child's voice, just a kid's.

I look up at Pigeon. Pigeon. He has a feeling about him that's big and almost like a man. And I can feel it all beginning again, now he's home. The story starts moving, and I can't stop it.

"Da ni am fynd lawr dre, Efa," I call to my sister, and it's not my mouth that says it. It doesn't feel like me.

151

Efa comes through, nods. She'll let me do anything. But this time Efa gives me a kiss, and in my ear, "Be careful, Iola," she says, but she lets me go anyway. Efa'll let me go anywhere, even down to the bus stops in town, where there's smoking and drinking and lads who can't keep their hands or their thoughts to themselves.

It's not until we're on the road on our own, Pigeon's white face glowing with the streetlights, that we say anything else.

"So be 'nes di'n Lerpwl?"

"In Liverpool? Nothing. We were shut in. I didn't do anything."

Pigeon, in English?

I try again. "'Ma raid nes ti 'wbath."

"Nope, not much." This Pigeon's a book full of blank pages.

"O," I say.

There's a long silence. I want to go back to mine, pretend he never came back.

"You stayin' at your mam's?" I ask him.

"Yep."

We walk down the hill in the yellow glow of the streetlamps.

Pigeon's different. And, although he came round, it's like he's come looking for something that isn't here anymore. Something we've lost, like Nain's ring which got lost in the laundry all those years back, and which we never found again although we all cursed black and blue looking for it. *It must be here. It must be here.* Like that. The same feeling of desperate, hopeless searching, except worse. Like losing your own eyes, or your ears, or your heart. I try twice more.

"Sut ma' dy fam?"

"She's alright."

"Ti, 'di gweld Cher?"

"Yep, she's at my house."

He stops, turns to look at me.

"Cher's staying in the shed now," he says. We scuff along the road, carrying on as if nothing's happened, as if Cher's the enemy. As if Cher's still pretty and clever and a girl everyone likes.

I stop. I feel sick to my stomach at the thought of it, my friend Cher, in that cold damp shed. It's not made for her. It's made for someone wild like Pigeon. Efa's word for him pops into my head. *Feral.* That's what she called him. Feral. Like one of the scraggy black cats that hang about by our door, waiting for scraps and love. Comfort. You have to turn them away, or they come back and back.

"Pigeon," I say, in English now, "I've just remembered I'm meeting someone, I've got to go."

Pigeon stands looking at me, as if I'm something he doesn't believe.

"Welai chdi eto rywbryd ta?" I say then in Welsh, to pretend we're still friends.

"Yep, see you," agrees Pigeon, standing still.

I walk away quickly, going right and going left between the houses and to my front door. Behind me Pigeon stands under the streetlight, pocketed hands, scuffed toes, green cat eyes looking after me, hungry.

Cher's waiting by my back door, she's standing there, could have waited for hours.

"He's back," she tells me.

"I know," I say, all innocent.

"Pigeon. He came back yesterday."

"I know, Cher."

I watch my friend's face.

"Don't look so happy, Cher."

"No," Cher agrees. "No," she says again, looking at the ground.

There's a silence. Then "He won't talk to me," I say.

"You saw him?"

"Yep."

"When?"

"Just now. But he won't talk."

"What, not at all?" asks Cher, slowly.

"Just not properly. Not in Welsh."

Cher looks confused.

"So?"

"I dunno. It's weird."

"You and me talk English," says Cher, shrugging her shoulders as if it doesn't matter.

I look at Cher, and there's that feeling. That feeling that it does matter. It matters a whole place worth of words and meanings and memories.

"What's he been doing?" Cher asks me.

"Dunno. Won't say."

"He's been somewhere bad, Iola," Cher says, seriously. "That's what it is. He doesn't want to think about it."

Sometimes Cher's clever again. Sometimes it's like she's going back to normal.

"He's moved my stuff out to the shed," she says. She says it with a big smile. As if it's a good thing.

"Cher that's terrible," I say.

"Why?" she says.

"It's cold and damp in there. It's not a place for someone to sleep!"

She looks at me like I'm mad.

"I always wanted to be allowed in," she says, as if I'm the

stupid one, "And now I am. I'm allowed the shed. And Pigeon has the house."

Poor Cher. She's so thick sometimes. And then other times she's so clever I think she knows it all.

We follow the path down to school, carrying on as if nothing's happened, as if nothing's ever happened, as if there's nothing wrong, and as if I've got all the right in the world to my life and my marks at school, and Cher doesn't and that's why she's got just a shed.

It's a couple of long, plain weeks before Pigeon comes to my house again. The next time I see him, it's on the anniversary of when Gwenllian, my mam, died. No one else thinks about the date anymore. Not even Efa. Especially not Efa who won't let me speak about either Gwenllian or our dad, but I remember the date every year. Seventh of May. I learnt it. It says it on the stone in the graveyard and so I learnt it, and I remember every year. I usually go there, to see her although I don't have much to say to her. She didn't stick around for long did she? She didn't properly meet me, and I didn't properly meet her. How can you miss someone you didn't know? It doesn't make sense. But I do. I miss her so much it's like not being able to breathe. Not like with Dad. With Dad I'm angry. He left on purpose.

I'm just about to head out to see Gwenllian when Pigeon arrives at the door. There's a feeling of things sinking suddenly, in a way I can't stop. Efa and Dafydd are out, and the house suddenly feels hollow without them. Pigeon comes in this time and then sits down on the sofa as if he belongs here and is just slotting himself into place. Pigeon has a strange weight to him, and everything seems to give for him, shift around to make space. This time he's more like the old

Pigeon. He's got this notebook, starts making notes. He's copying out what's in the newspaper Efa's left open on the table. He's always done this. He copies something out, and then he'll change the order of it. I used to think it was just a bit of fun. Now it feels like Pigeon wants to take everything, learn it, and change it all around. Why can't he ever just let things be?

"Why d'you hang round with Cher?" he says, in English again, still copying as he asks me. He doesn't even look up.

"She's alright"

"She's a freak.'"

"Nacdi tad, cau hi," I say, half sticking up for her, but not in a strong and brave way. Not like a friend should.

"Anyways, she's a lesbo," he says, with a chuckle.

When did he start just calling people lazy names? Scumbag. Lesbo. Before, he'd make up stories, and then the names'd come after. Now it was just names. Empty names in fake English.

"Shut up, Pigeon," I say then, as if he'd never been away. As if we're pals who can afford to argue. He gets a black look.

"Are *you* a lesbo?"

"No." I feel the heat in my face.

He grins "D'you fancy me then?"

"No." My face burns even more.

"Bet you do really."

"Don't."

"I've gotta girlfriend, anyway."

"You have not." My face cools too quick. Something icy in my stomach.

"Do so."

"Be di 'i henw hi ta?"

"Ceri."

"No way." Ceri's in my class. She's got boobs, a bad attitude.

"Yes way." he grins. "Anyway, can I borrow a book?"

It takes me by surprise. So I don't answer for a few seconds, just sit there staring at him.

"Which book?" I say eventually.

"I dunno." He looks at me and then he says, "One about a murder maybe?" with a smile.

The words are like quick hail. I'm up, and walking out, leaving Pigeon all alone in my own house.

I need to walk. My shoes are hard and regular on the road and the road's solid. I walk. I walk up the steep street, up the hillside. At the top you can see the mountains tumbling down towards you, all draped with clouds. I walk up for a time that's not countable, and then turn to skirt the hill and all along, past the estate, and down the river which is swelled up with spring and decorated with green plants growing fast and lush and too full of life. I walk the path by the river, then the other path, the one to the graveyard by the church.

The graveyard's where Gwenllian's buried. She's five rows up and two rows in. There's some dead chrysanthemums in a pot by the grave. Did Efa bring them? I stand there looking at the stone. It says Gwenllian. My mam's name. Gwenllian.

I don't know much about her. Only that Dad loved her, and she died just after I was born, and then he obviously didn't care so much about us, Efa and me, because he left us then, with Nain and her rules and tellings off.

I think, stood in front of this Gwenllian's grave, that it's a shame I never knew her, cos, with a name like that, she must've been a story.

I pick up the dead chrysanthemums then, and I say, "Ta ta Gwenllian," and start walking back home to Efa.

When I get home I find Pigeon's left a note for me and Efa, scrawled on the back of a newspaper, saying he's borrowed a book, but he'll bring it back. And it's not Agatha Christie or any of Efa's other murder books. It's a children's book full of old-fashioned stories, by Hans Christian Andersen.

Efa thinks it's funny.

"What on earth does he want with that?" she says.

What would Pigeon want with children's stories?

27

He'd thought he was after something scientific. He was after something that was full of FACTS and experiments and explaining things just the way they were. And then he got to that row of bright spines. They were all picture books there, for kids. He got one off the shelf. This was the kind of thing Iola would've read when she was little. He opened this one. It was a big blue book, quite heavy. It was for a mam or a dad to read to you, it'd be too heavy for a small kid to hold on their own. He sat down on the sofa. Iola's sofa. Next to him there was a pile of clothes, waiting to be ironed or folded and to be put away. He could smell something vinegary coming from the kitchen. It was probably pickle. There was always something on the go in Iola's house. Efa was always doing something, cleaning or cooking or lighting candles, or listening to music. In his house there was just mam. She hardly moved all day. They watched TV in his house. They ate food from packets and tins. In Iola's house there was always things happening, people working to make things happen. It made things move around inside you. You were like the house. Going places. Happening. Pigeon sat on the sofa next to the clothes that were halfway through being folded, smelling the pickle that was halfway to being made. Iola'd be back in a minute. Perhaps she'd be angry? Or was she scared? He'd better just get a book and go, come back another day. Why'd he said that thing to her? Said 'about a murder'. Why'd he said it?

He sits with the big book, and he starts to read. And the first lines of the story are like visiting an old house in the past where things are different and where people wash clothes on a Saturday and make their own bread. It's old fashioned, the story, and it has a taste like a cinnamon bun, spicy and sweet and gone out of fashion.

It's because of the words. The words aren't for him, they're for someone else. Someone with tidy, ironed trousers, round cheeks, and a mam who wears scarves, has pink, soft lips, smells clean. "Once upon a time," she says, and she smiles. Pigeon closes the book.

But he never gets a science book, a book about facts, instead he takes the story book, leaves by the back door, and goes over the gardens and hedges and walls until he gets to his house.

From the side wall, he can see that there's a man standing on the front doorstep.

Pigeon stands back, and watches the man knock on his door, he skirts around the side of the house to the front, and, as he walks up to the man, the door opens, and his mam stands there. She's not wearing proper clothes. She's wearing a nightie. She shouldn't be opening the door to a man in just that. She's too pretty. He watches from the gate. But his mam sees Pigeon, and, just when the man's leaning down to her in a way that turns his stomach, she says quickly "I can't do this now. Come back tomorrow."

The man leans towards her still, as if he's going to kiss her but then he doesn't. He touches her on her hip, and walks away. That touch, as if he owned her.

"Who're you?" asks Pigeon, but the man only looks at him briefly and walks away. He doesn't answer. He doesn't even answer. The man looks familiar. How does Pigeon know him? How?

"Is that your boyfriend?" Pigeon asks her as she shuts the door after him. But when she turns round she's pale, and she looks full of upset and tears.

"No," she says, shaking her head.

"But he touched you."

"Yes," she said, "he did."

She faces him.

"Pigeon, with Him gone and Cher to look after and all. I needed the money."

He stares at her. What does she mean?

"I needed his money," she says. Then she sits down hard. "And the others," she says, looking down.

Pigeon stares at her. The others? Money? Then it's as if the whole room is suddenly swimming in a queasy green light. His mam, sat there, in her nightie. His mam now, standing, saying "Pigeon!" the lipstick around her mouth making the shape of his name. Then he pushes past her and out of the house again.

It's not until he's up the hill, above the town, looking down at the strewn houses and fields and the layered streets, that he knows it. That man touching his mam had been the same one watching Iola's window.

And that's when he gets it, Pigeon. He'll need to be the one in control, here, in this town full of liars and cheats and people who want to run you into the ground. You're either a winner or a loser. And being a winner is all about keeping your doors and windows closed to the wrong people. Being a winner means being the one who held the gun, who killed Him, who calls the shots, has the key to his own front door, and has the force to keep it closed.

28

I walk back home from school the long way, along the path that goes up the valley with the river, where there's all the pools the kids from town come to, to swim. You can hear them now, the sounds of laughing and splashing around and the gasps as they jump in. The water's freezing, since it's only the beginning of May.

I walk round the bend in the river, coming up to the waterfall that's like a paradise in the spring. There's all the green rocks and trees round the waterfall, and there's a perfect pool at the bottom. The water squirms down into it. That's when I see them, Pigeon and his girlfriend, sat by the waterfall. They've probably been there all day. Pigeon doesn't do school and I don't think she's too bothered either.

Pigeon's grabbing Ceri all over and kissing her. It's disgusting.

I stand watching. I stand watching their twisting bodies until he pulls away and says something to Ceri and stands up.

I start walking away, but then turn again because I can hear Ceri's voice rising.

"You're an idiot if you do that, Pigeon. It's too high. It's not deep enough!"

Pigeon's stripped down to his shorts, and while Ceri and me watch he climbs right up to the top of the rock, and he looks down at the pool. There's only three'll do that jump. Three of the boys in town.

I'm not keen. I don't like it when they do it. The pool's a long way below, and it's not that deep. A boy got injured last year. It was just his arm. *Luckily,* Efa'd said.

Watching Pigeon, stood in his shorts, and his white, thin body with the pale light that comes through the trees making shapes on him, my hands are hot and sweaty and I feel that sickness, that old familiar sickness that comes when Pigeon's getting in trouble. I don't want him to jump. I don't.

I shout it, without meaning to, "Stopia! Pigeon, Stopia!" and he looks at me. And he looks at me, and he jumps.

But he's alright, Pigeon, swimming in the pool after jumping off the rock. He's cold, and shouting with the cold, and then, when he's used to it a bit he's laughing at me and Ceri who're both stood with our hands on our mouths looking terrified. He's swimming and doing rolly-pollys in the water, and he looks different, down there in that pool. He looks happy. And it makes me think about that question the police asked me, in that cold room after it all happened, when they were trying to work it all out.

"Do you think Pigeon's unhappy?" they asked.

I never answered.

He was happy when we used to go up into the old quarries exploring all the holes and the mountains of slate, where, if you fell, you might've plunged all the way down the slate tips, and landed cut to pieces at the bottom. He was happy when we used to go to the tops of the hill nearest town too, running up one in front of the other past the cows and over the stiles, and up the side of the steep hill and along the bumpy spine of it until we got right to the top, with no breath left in us at all, and too cold in the wind but it was so worth it.

Because there you could look down on everything like it was a rucked-up blanket, and all the fields and the sky and even sometimes clouds were below us, and there below us we'd see my house, and we'd see Pigeon's house, where He lived, and Pigeon'd spit at it. Spit at the crooked, ugly house that was supposed to be his home. And then we'd laugh, Pigeon and me, we'd laugh. And I'd try to spit as far as Pigeon could. But I'd never manage it.

Pigeon was happy then, and right now, swimming in the pool, he's happy too.

Ceri sits on the rock, watching Pigeon. She doesn't say anything. Pigeon ignores Ceri and he just swims down there, round in circles in the pool for ages, although it must be freezing, and he ignores me too, stood up here watching him. Ceri just hangs about.

After a while Pigeon climbs out of the water, and he shakes all over like a dog, and he goes back to Ceri, cos he wants to cop a feel, and probably cos he's cold and blue and white and she's all warm and soft. And that's when I leave, I leave the two of them to it.

"Bye, Iola," he shouts, as I go round the corner. His voice spreads behind me, clear and too real.

I don't answer, wish he'd say it in Welsh, wish he'd speak to me again, really speak to me as if none of this has happened. But it has happened. It's happened to him. What I did has happened to him. He's made a real life of it. Faced it, and he's living it anyway. So he can jump into that pool, and live, and not go to school and just mark time like I do.

There's part of me that thinks that. It was me. Part of me that thinks that. And then this other part. It was him.

Perhaps he can't talk anymore even if he tried? I had that dream again last night. Pigeon, with no mouth. With just skin where the mouth should be.

29

It's a funny thing, that right beside the grey town there's places like magic. There's mountains like fists coming out of the land, their rocky tops as raw and rough as a cruel man's knuckles. There's rivers. In the rivers all the rain gathers like a riot. Like a stampede. And then there's still, quiet places, like the pool.

Pigeon can't remember ever being held before. Ceri's arms are like a warm bath, and she's soft. He wants Ceri. He wants her like a child wants. But he wants her like a man wants too.

Because her words are so hard, they don't speak much. What have they got to say to each other? But her arms and her body are like a warm, comfortable bed, and he wants to be near her, and to be touched. He wants her too much. In too many different ways. He wants her. He doesn't care who she is. He wants her to fill the spaces left between things.

"Coming down the arcades?" she asks. Her voice is a bored voice. It's the voice of a big kid, who's bored sitting by the river, a kid who wouldn't understand how Pigeon feels.

"Maybe after," he says.

Her dad owns the arcades. They get free goes on some of the machines, but it's dark in the arcades, and shut in, and her dad's there so Pigeon can't touch Ceri, and then she's nothing and he always thinks why is he there at all?

"After what?"

He's quiet a minute, after what?

"After this!" he says taking off his shirt and standing above the still pool on the rock. It's like it's all going to end when you jump. That's why you do it. If he misses, or jumps too deep...

And then there she is, Iola, stood watching. Stood watching him. Is she following him? Like before. Is she following him like before? But when he looks at her she's got an expression on her face, watching him, and she doesn't want him to jump.

When he gets home from the river, going to the house is like going underground into a cave where there's no light. Cher's outside in the shed. It's just his mam now. She's sitting in the living room, crying. Someone must've been here. Pigeon feels it. The anger. Someone has been in his house. Another man. Pigeon feels it again, that feeling, of gasping for air. When he moves closer, to comfort her, he sees that her wrists are red, and she keeps touching her neck. He lifts her hair from her neck and he sees the redness there too. He tries opening the windows, but it doesn't work. The house is still dark, it still smells of people shut in. It smells like dust and there's this heavy feeling when he sits next to his mam, watches her as she rocks, and listens as she half sings a hymn, and then a lullaby.

Then he remembers the book. He takes it out of the drawer. "Once upon a time," he says. The words sound borrowed in his mouth. What does it mean? Once upon a time? He sits next to her. He opens the book to the first page. "Once upon a time," he says before he begins, because that's what you're supposed to say. Pigeon tries to remember what it was like, back then, when he could make up a story, make up something good. His mam looks up, surprised. She smiles at Pigeon then, smiles at him as he begins to tell her a story where it will all be alright. A fairytale. Makebelieve. But Pigeon just begins to read to her.

"Far, far from land, where the waters are as blue as the petals of the cornflower and as clear as glass," he takes a breath, the words in the room sound difficult and strange, but they do, they let light in. "There," he reads again, "where no anchor can reach the bottom."

30

Gwyn Gelataio is doing 'Return to Learning'. On a Monday morning, he gets up in the bleary-eyed little flat he's renting above the chip shop on the quay, inserting first one short leg and then the other into his blue jeans, pulling them up around his wide waist, and, with a little bob curtsy, doing up his flies.

"Ah," he says, for no reason but habit.

In the fire, Gwyn lost his magazines, his sofa, a bedroom's worth of furniture, many mod cons from the kitchen, and, crucially, the portrait of his mother – disapproval curling around her brow like a vice as the flames licked devilishly at her.

Miraculously surviving the blaze, the glass-topped coffee table and the greying plastic flowers, slightly wilted in the heat, were now the only reminders of his mother's dreams for him. Emerging from a cloud of beige, smoke clearing his lungs, free for the first time from the ambition-by-proxy of his mother's expectations, and in receipt of a never-dreamed-of windfall which had come bountifully from both the home insurance and the compensation awarded by the court, Gwyn found himself dreaming of a new life, and then, much to his surprise, suddenly skipping through the flow-chart-bullet-point-step-by-step world of career advice, job seminars, college open days, and evening classes, childlike and curious for the first time in his life.

Not knowing what to study, Gwyn had first made his way through a battery of GCSE courses, from Maths to English, to Cookery to French (despite his Italian boy's headstart in romance languages, strangely acing the Cookery and failing the French) and then, still unable to decide, he had done a part-time Access course in art, constructing a monumental ice-cream cone from cardboard boxes. The work was dedicated to the loving memory of his late mother, who, no doubt, grumbled huffily from her grave that "Gwiiiin, you are awasting your atime with this aaaaarrrt raaabish" whilst Gwyn's cone happily gave her the finger.

The art thing was cathartic, and therefore short-lived. Gwyn, the ice-cream man, it turned out, thrived on subjects even more morbid than art. The legacy of his days as a boring bachelor in need of a thrill was an enduring fascination with the bloodcurdling antiheroes he came across in the film adaptations of novels by Easton Ellis, Harris and King. So perhaps it was because of them, rather than because of any pervasive sense of victimhood, that the placid Gwyn, scuttling from his blatant failure on the art course, finally settled on psychology.

An uncertain pass at A level psychology was squeezed out of him by Megan, his rather touchy-feely tutor, via long, late-night personal tutorials. During these late-night sessions, Megan induced him, finally, to question the strange events of those few months, which had led not only to his wonderful period of homelessness, but also, tragically, to the serious injury of that little girl.

"But *why*?" Megan said over and over. "We have to think

why? Why why why? Why did they do it?" shaking her head, and leaning towards him, eyelashes batting frantically.

Gwyn remembered the girl's words, just before she launched at him, biting and kicking, and those words, or rather *that* word 'Murderer', repeated again by the little gremlins as they broke his kitchen window. The rolling syllables of it still played on his mind like a dodgy remix.

If Megan left satisfied (in the kind of way you're satisfied unimpressively by a poor petrol-station sandwich), Gwyn was left in a state of panic. Questioning things (his mother, the justice system, his place in life) had never been Gwyn Gelataio's natural mode, and the new habit left things uncomfortably misshaped somehow.

Immediately following the fire, Gwyn had been so concerned with living arrangements, so shocked by the total life change that had befallen him, and so amazed by his new sex life, as, unimpinged by his mother's gate-keeping, first one middle-aged woman and then another offered him a place on their sofa, and then in their bed, that he had breezed thoughtlessly through the process of filing a statement for the police and attending the juvenile courts at Pigeon's tribunal, and had not even bothered to stay to find out how the boy was sentenced. Since Pigeon refuted his argument that there were two children present in Mrs Gelataio's stagnant flat on that smoke-filled Sunday, Gwyn had withdrawn that part of his statement with not so much as a blink, not really being interested in justice, retribution or revenge. In fact he felt profoundly indebted to the thin boy with the green eyes who sat there on the video link, so slight and pale in the echoing chamber of righteous adults.

Having been a lonely, smothered child whose life was utterly devoid of play, Gwyn's new experiences – as he studied in an ugly polytechnic, made choices, explored the fairytale freedom of friendships, of playing at sex – gave him new reference points. *Fun* was one. *Imagination* also had begun to simmer weakly, and *Escape* lingered at the edges of awareness too. These three co-ordinates threw the children's actions, their high little voices and their schemes and plots into new relief. So, as he sits on the toilet this Monday morning before college, playing that word, the child's echoing accusation, "Murderer. Murderer. Llofrudd," over and over in his head yet again, Gwyn finally recognises the demon-vandal-pigeon-boy for a child. He re-appraises those pale little faces, those eyes, the voices shrieking "Murderer! Llofrudd!" that have given him so many sleepless nights, and, for the first time Gwyn recognises Pigeon and Iola's little game as fairytale, fable, as pushing toy cars across a deep-pile carpet, or fighting imaginary dinosaurs on the sofa. Gwyn sees Pigeon's pale face, his scared green eyes, and sees a boy caught in a web of make-believe gone wrong.

31

It's half term, and there's nothing to do except look out of the window and think about boys. But I don't want to think about Llion anymore. I don't want to think about him. Llion's just dry hands and wanting what I don't want to give him. And Llion's another person who doesn't care anyway. I hang out of the bedroom window, looking down over the grey town, and over at the mountains where the clouds move as if they're gobbling at the craggy tops of the hills. The wind that blows down from the hills is cold and fresh and like the slap in the face I need.

"Iola! Close that window will you? It's blowing a gale!" shouts Efa from downstairs. I go to close it.

Wait. From here at the window I can see a man walking up the road that whooshes up the hill like a muscle. He's walking all on his own on the road, the wind like a brushstroke pulling him along. I see his short little legs and the top of his bald head, and I don't even have to see his face with its bristly shadows to know that it's Gwyn! Poor Gwyn.

And then I see, stood there, there on the road by the streetlight just a few meters away from Gwyn, there's *Pigeon!* And I want to shout out at one or both of them *Gofalwch! Be careful, Murderer! Murderer!* It takes me by surprised that I want to shout that. So stupid. As if part of me still believes it.

But I don't. So I just peer out from the window, and watch Gwyn walking up to Pigeon, watch while his arm comes out, stretching out in front of him, like he's going to give Pigeon something with his hand, and my heart is almost stopping just to see them standing there. And the two of them almost the same height too.

And it's then I see what they're doing: shaking hands, like men do, like men do in meetings between men. Proper and grown up. Dignified.

I realise it properly, watching him. What we did to him, with his ice-cream van and all that, was terrible. What we burnt was his life. And that is a serious, grown-up thing to do to someone, something even adults would be ashamed of, and would hide forever. It doesn't run out. It sticks. And I hate Pigeon, I hate him, standing down there with Gwyn, having their unknown, unimaginable conversation, because it was all him. All him, but it's my fault in a deep, private way, that no one knows, a secret that's closing me up like a bud that won't open.

The young man, standing in my window frame, shaking hands, has come clean. Pigeon's been punished already. Everyone knows about Pigeon, and what Pigeon did – to Gwyn and to Cher – and Pigeon can just kind of wear what he's done wrong, like it's not him, it's just something that belongs to him, like jeans or a jumper or baseball boots. He can wear it, and not keep it buried and black. So he can look Gwyn in the eye, shake his hand, say "I'm sorry" like a good loser. He can tell everyone he was bad before, and now he's good, and he's sorry and he's learnt his lesson.

I hate him.

I need to go down there and tell Gwyn it was me. I did it. I need to make Pigeon let me tell him. I grab my coat, open my bedroom door.

I hesitate though, because Efa and Dafydd are down there in the living room. I don't want them to see me crying. I open my door to check they're still there.

"What've you been doing?" Efa's saying to Dafydd, down in the living room. "You've got bruises all up your arms."

This stops me. I stand and listen. I'd noticed them too and wondered if he'd been fighting. They reminded me of Pigeon's, years ago. I want to know about the bruises. The full story. They could be bad news for me and Efa, like He was bad news.

"Oh, you know," says Dafydd. "Gardening."

"Gardening?!" says Efa, not believing a word. She's not thick, Efa.

"Have you thought that maybe Pigeon and Iola don't think of each other just as friends any more?" says Dafydd quickly.

I hold still, push my door open a thin slice further. Through the door and through the pine banisters I can see Dafydd down in the lounge, sitting back easily on the sofa as if it's his, his eyes tracing the headline of the front page like he's following a fly walking across the paper. His slippers are half off his heels and his dressing gown is open some, showing the black hairs that walk like ants all over him. It's funny, having a man in the house. The man of the house, Efa calls him. Efa was the man of the house before.

"Why d'you say that?" Efa bends to her stitching, gathering a fresh bit of cloth to the quilt and working her deft hands to pull the thread in out, in out, with the needle.

"Just an observation." Dafydd stops in that way when

176

you're trying to decide if you should say something. Or maybe he already knows. It's like he's being dramatic.

"I caught him watching her the other day," he says then. He doesn't even look up from the paper he's reading to say it. He takes a swig of coffee, lets what he's said rise through the room. Behind the door, I feel sick. *Pigeon's watching me?* He's following me. He'll never let me go.

"Watching?" Efa's hands hover a moment. She's turned her face away from Dafydd, so that I can see her expression but he can't. Even from up here I can see how her brow moves, sinking to make that dip between her eyes.

"Yep, from the garden, watching her window, little scumbag."

What he's saying sinks in.

"Don't call him that," says Efa quickly. She's always liked Pigeon, Efa. Doesn't matter what he's done, she likes him. When you say anything about him she gets that soft look in her eye, the look she used to keep for me.

Dafydd sighs. "Anyway, it's a bit out of order. Want me to have a word?"

"No, just leave it, they're teenagers that's all." Efa takes up another piece of cloth, lines it up with the first. Dafydd looks at her. He's got this expression. He wants something.

"I know, I know, but he's sneaky, y'know? Coming in and taking that book like that. And then, look at what he did. He's criminal." Dafydd's put down the paper, his voice is whiny like a kid's.

"It's not that simple, Dafydd. Poor Pigeon. He had a hell of a time." Efa's eyebrows twitch.

"Well, he probably deserved it." Dafydd says it just under his breath, but it's that kind of whisper that even I can hear.

"Dafydd!"

"Yeah, yeah, I know."

"Dafydd."

"Alright. Alright. I don't trust him though." He stands up, his dressing gown falling open so that I look away.

"Glass of wine? You off the detox?" he asks Efa.

"Nope, not til Friday." Efa's head moves for no. "And anyway you're a big phoney: telling the whole class you were going to keep it up for a month!"

"It's the depth of the process, not the length that counts." Dafydd sounds like a proper idiot striding off to the kitchen, his slippers clipping along the floor.

Efa, left on the sofa, looks after him and rolls her eyes. Then she spots me standing listening at the half-open door at the top of the stairs. She looks me in the eye then. It's a long look. What does it mean? There's the sound of a glass of wine being poured, and Dafydd comes back through, dangling the neck of the glass between his long fingers. He sits with a grumbling look. Efa doesn't say anything about me watching. She ignores me, bends to work on her patchwork quilt, symbolising love, the family, peace, and stuff like that. I go back into my room. And sit on the bed. Stuck.

32

It was with a measure of guilt that Gwyn decided, yesterday, to look up the boy. He trawled through directories, racking his brain for Pigeon's surname, and finally, when that failed, traipsed up the long-forgotten hill in the rain to question the old ladies about the grey little boy with the green eyes, who'd been sent away for killing, and follow their spindly pointing fingers along and down and around the houses until he was pointed straight to the helter-skelter house, and rapped its rattly door.

Gwyn was astonished by the beautiful spectre of a woman that answered the door. They stared at each other, Mari half hidden behind the door, both lost for words. Stammering "Ydi Pigeon yma?" and getting only a lost headshake in reply, Gwyn could only leave a note for the boy in Mari's trembling hand as she stood stupefied in the doorway, haloed by greying auburn hair and surrounded by the stench of lost dreams.

This message stayed grasped tight in her fist until that night when Pigeon, brushing his mother's hair, noticed the roughened scrap of paper in her hand, and unfurled her fingers from around it, like the fronds of a fern.

Now, walking towards the boy, tall as he was, thin, almost

an adult, it is with the greatest of self-control that Gwyn manages to suppress the hysterical Italian inside from eschewing the ritual handshake and giving Pigeon a big bear hug and a sloppy kiss on the cheek. A lump rises in Gwyn's throat and something like hope starts to make a shape of Pigeon's pale mouth, and to soften his angry almost man's eyes. The two hands meet soberly, as Iola watches, as the streetlights dimly glow on the side of the hill, as Efa makes her quilt downstairs, and as, back along the road, Pigeon's mother hums a sea shanty under her hanging dresses in the dark of their wobbly house, while all around them all the town sits down to meat and two veg and television stories.

"I'm sorry," says Pigeon. He says the little word with a shrug. He almost smiles. Gwyn grins. The word is comic against all this.

"Oh," Gwyn says, thinking *why is the boy speaking English?* "That's OK. It didn't really matter."

"We burnt your house!" says Pigeon. Looking at Gwyn as if he's off his rocker.

Gwyn nods. He grins again.

"It wasn't such a bad thing," he says, sincerely. "I needed a fresh start."

Pigeon's looking at him. He laughs grimly. "I know what you mean," he says.

"Anyway," says Gwyn. "I'm sorry you got sent away."

"I killed someone," says Pigeon. There's a kind of fragile pride when he says it.

Gwyn nods. "From what I hear," he says, "he was a nasty piece of work."

Pigeon says nothing.

"How long've you been home?"

"A couple of months," Pigeon shrugs again.

"Are you at school then?"

"Nope."

"College?"

Pigeon shakes his head.

"Have you got a job then? Oh sorry," says Gwyn, realising the boy's probably unemployed.

"Sort of," says Pigeon. "I sort of have a job."

"Oh good," says Gwyn. "Good."

They stand there awkwardly.

"Can I tell you a secret?" asks Pigeon.

Gwyn nods, a bit nervously. What's the boy up to?

"It wasn't me."

"What d'you mean?"

"I mean, I didn't do it."

"The fire?" Gwyn knows that's not true. "I saw you," he says, shaking his head.

"Oh no. Not that," says Pigeon, waving his hand dismissively "I mean the murder."

Gwyn looks at him. The lad's still got a screw loose.

"Anyway," says Gwyn quickly, "Must be going." What had he been hoping to achieve anyway?

"She did it," said Pigeon suddenly.

Gwyn didn't even have to ask who. He knew. That pale child with the eyes. The one he'd removed from his statement. That small lie by omission. Gwyn walked away, down the road as quick as his short legs could carry him.

33

Maybe it was seeing him with Gwyn. Or maybe it's the book: Hans Christian Anderson. Pigeon? That big gap between them. Like two sides of a whole world. I don't know. Or maybe it's the jump he made into that pool. The cold feeling I had, of not wanting him to. And the terrible fear as I heard him slice the water. Or maybe it *is* what Dafydd said? Dafydd's thin voice, telling Efa about Pigeon. About Pigeon watching me. It could be any of these things. But I think all of them boil down to one: Pigeon is what everything's about. He's in the middle of everything. And even though him being back ties a knot in my stomach so tight I can barely breathe, I missed him when he wasn't here. When he wasn't here, running along the wet streets, or collecting things in endless piles of memories, or telling stories which hiss and bubble, or causing trouble. I missed him. Like an arm or a leg. Or a mouth, if it was suddenly gone. So when Cher calls round to go shopping together, I tell I'll see her later up at the quarry, and I go to call on Pigeon.

It's smaller than it was, his house, crouched on the street between other houses, and uglier than it was too. And when I go to the door, the new, pristine PVC door, I feel suddenly sick, and in my head there's echoing sounds. In my head can hear crying and shouting and someone being hit, I can hear someone shouting *No!* and the sound of a shot. I have to sit on the front step and get my breathing back to normal. This isn't the first time I've heard those things. Like a nightmare that repeats. Repeats.

Since He's not there anymore, I go to the proper house, not to the shed, and I knock. The knock sounds wrong. A long word comes into my head. In-ap-pro-pri-ate. Inappropriate. Pigeon pulls the door open, doesn't even say hello, walks along the corridor to the sitting room, expecting me to follow. It's as if it was only yesterday I was here.

"Sut mae?" I say to his mam in the living room.

I might as well be talking to myself. His mam doesn't say anything back. She sits sewing in one corner of the dark room. I think of her, properly, for the first real time, look closely at her sewing hands, thin and pale as they are, and see that they're going over and over one bit of material and that what she's doing doesn't make any sense. She's carefully stitched closed all the openings of the dress, closing the neckline, closing the holes for your arms, closing the hemline along the bottom, so nobody can get into the dress, and nobody can get out.

Pigeon sits at the other side of the room. Pigeon lights a cigarette. Still smoking?

I feel relieved that Pigeon's still smoking. It's like the old Pigeon. The old Pigeon before what happened, before what he did, what I did, what we did together.

Pigeon's mam puts her sewing down, and starts humming a song to herself, sitting in the dark in the corner, rocking. A drink, whisky or brandy, sits cloudy in the glass by her side. It's a lullaby she's singing,

si hei lwli lwli lws
si hei lwli lwli lws

I recognise it as one of Nain's. It's funny to think of Nain ever singing a lullaby. I remember her singing it, neatly, and in a matter of fact way. But Pigeon's mam sings it differently. It makes me think of sad things to hear it.

Pigeon goes and gets the radio from upstairs and switches it on to drown her out. The static fills the room until he tunes it to a football match and the crowd's cheers that rise and fall like a sea thrashing. He doesn't say anything to me. He ignores me. Or is he waiting for me to speak? His mam ignores me too. It's like she's not there. I sit down on the sofa as if I'm nothing.

"Efa's boyfriend's a scumbag," says Pigeon suddenly.

"No, he's not," I say quickly, because Dafydd's the man of our house. He's our man.

"He is," says Pigeon.

Why does he say this? There's something about the way he says it, makes me think I don't want to know.

Pigeon goes to the cabinet in the corner, gets the square bottle, fills his mam's glass. She looks up at him, all vague, stops in her song.

"Iola," says Pigeon into the silence, looking at me suddenly "D'you think it was my fault, what happened to Cher?"

The question kicks the wind out of me. I can't breathe. There's a long silence. When I speak, my voice is raw and low.

"Na, Pigeon. No way. Gwyn did it. You know that."

"Gwyn?"

"Well it was his fault anyway, that the van fell." My voice sounds tiny, and stupid, like a kid's.

There's a long silence. Pigeon pulls another cigarette from

his packet. He goes to the kitchen and lights it from the stove. He comes back, stands by the door.

"Who hurt Cher, Iola?"

"Dwn im ... I dunno," I shrug. I don't want to look at him.

Pigeon walks close to me, sits down next to me on the sofa, puts his cigarette to smoke itself in the ashtray, and reaches for one of my wrists so that I have to turn to him.

"We did, Iola." He says it so quietly that I know it's what he believes. I'm shaking my head. But he's going on. "We made the whole thing up, and then we hurt her, Iola. We did it cos we hated her, didn't we Iola? We did it."

There's a long silence. He's holding both my wrists now, not holding hard, quite gently, but holding. It's a long time before I can speak. But then I do. I find a voice somewhere, one that comes up from my ribs, from where the heaviness is.

"Na Pigeon, ti'n wrong. It was a mistake, Cher got hurt cos she made a mistake, that's all, just kids Pigeon, kids."

When I say that word 'kids', so English and so adult, it's like I'm dressing up in Efa's grown-up clothes again. I feel small suddenly. I'm a kid. I'm still a kid. Somewhere I still am.

"We almost killed her, Iola." Pigeon's hands hold tighter. He's not in control. His bony hands are holding my wrists so tight it hurts, and in my head there's that shouting again, that voice saying "Na!" and that sound of a shot.

"Stop saying that Pigeon, stopia Pigeon, paid a deud hyna, plis." My voice is so thin, so small against the room.

"Cher might've died."

"But she's alright. Efa said she'll be alright."

There's a long silence. Just the creak of his mam's chair and the radio sounds rising falling. Just the slow dwindling smoke of the left cigarette.

Pigeon pushes me away, gets up, walks across the room and slumps down in the armchair. He looks at me for a long time, and then there's his hard, tight voice.

"And what about Him, Iola?" says Pigeon's voice "What happened to Him?"

It's so foreign to hear that name, that terrifying emphasis. Him. I don't answer. Don't say anything at all. I want to say *you did it, Pigeon, ti nath,* but I can't. I say nothing. We both know. Even I know what happened, I can still hear it in my head.

Pigeon sits there and he says nothing at all. And then he beckons with a hand. *Come over here* says his hand.

"Pam, Pigeon?" But I think I know. I think I know why.

"Just come over, Iola. Come over here."

And I walk over to him, stand there in front of him where he's sitting in the chair. He stands up. And he puts a hand to the back of my neck and he pulls my face into him, and then his lips are cold, and hard and like a boy's.

He stops. He sits down in the chair again. I'm standing above him, looking down. And then Pigeon's shoulders are going up and down, up and down like he can't breathe, and like it hurts when he does, and it's like his whole body is full of something bad, and then I understand: this is what happens to Pigeon when he cries. He cries more, more than I am, more than I ever have. It's like a nightmare his crying, dirty and angry and not belonging in things that I know, and not making any sense.

"Pigeon, stop! It wasn't us Pigeon. It was something else. It was something else."

But he can't hear me. Even I can't really hear.

"Pigeon!" I say, shaking him, trying to stop him crying "Pigeon!" But Pigeon's curled up now on the armchair, curled up so tight on one side that I can't undo him, can't get him to look or talk, and the room's full of static from the radio again, all the cheering gone.

I need to go. I need to go home. I leave him there. And all I can hear while I leave the house is the sound of the cheering on the radio, and above it Pigeon's mam, still singing that lullaby ghost song.

si hei lwli lwli lws
si hei lwli lwli lws

34

After the crying there was a long empty time where Pigeon didn't think and was still, still, still in the dark room.

Slowly, he uncurled from the knot of the foetal position he'd been lying in on the chair. He sat up, propped his elbows on his knees and rested his head in his hands until the thoughts returned.

He didn't know why he'd said it. Why'd he even thought it then, when he was with Iola. Why'd he accused her of it? He didn't know.

He didn't know, wasn't conscious of it, of what had happened in the house all those years ago. It was blocked out. But when she came round, he suddenly felt it all, because she was there, in his house, like she'd been before. It was because she'd come to the door, and knocked, and come in.

Inappropriate.

It was a word Pigeon'd learnt all those years back. In-ap-pro-pri-ate. It sounded in his ears now, made a noise that was like an itch, and he wanted it out.

Now she was gone, the room was back to the way it was before. Shut in. Or shutting everything out. It was dark. It was empty except for his mam, him, breathing. There was just the one real thing in the room again. It was something to hold on to. It made it all worth it. That he'd done it. Got rid of Him.

He got up, went to the drawer, took the blue book out, and began to read. His voice dry, as if it was full of salt. His mouth was too dirty for the words, and too old. But he said them, and as he did, perhaps his mam stopped rocking so hard, perhaps the room slowed, and perhaps the light coming in through the window didn't have to push so hard through the dead air.

"The princesses," he began, reading slowly and clearly and perfectly from the blue book, "liked nothing better than to listen to their old grandmother tell about the world above."

He looked over at his mam. She was sitting quietly. Was she listening? Was he reading for her? He didn't know. He didn't know why he was reading. He was reading for the dark room, the old furniture, the dirty windows. He was reading to turn it all inside out. He took a deep breath, and went on.

"She had to recount countless times..."

He liked that, *recount countless times*.

That old feeling for storing words, the excitement of it, the secrecy nudged at him. He almost smiled.

"She had to recount countless times," he said again, "all she knew about ships, towns, human beings, and the animals that lived up on land. The youngest of the mermaids thought it particularly," he hesitated over the twists of the word, "par-ti-cu-lar-ly," he said again, "particu-larly wonderful that the flowers up there had fragrance, for they did not have on the bottom of the sea. She also liked to hear about the green forest, where the fishes that swam among the branches could sing most beautifully."

Pigeon stopped. He stopped to watch the light from the

window, from the second-hand sun. How it moved through the thick air in the room, as if it was moving through dank water, through a dirty fish tank.

"But," he said, focusing on the black letters, on his own mouth saying the words against the room, "the grandmother promised, 'when you are fifteen, then you will be allowed to swim to the surface. Then you can climb up on a rock and sit and watch the big ships sail by. If you dare, you can swim close enough to the shore to see the towns and the forest.' "

He stopped. He was fifteen.

He thought about it. This was a story about being a prisoner. This was a story about being inside. In a centre. In a house. In a shed. In a story. He closed the book, and sat watching the white light filtering into the room. It came over him again. He needed air. Air. Where was it? Where was the surface of all this? How did you breathe in it?

35

Efa is so worried about me when I arrive home shaking and pale that, after trying for a good while to find out what's wrong, she actually invites me to go to her class with her. I say yes to going straight away, because it's doing something with Efa and, right now, I want to be close to her again as much as I want to breathe.

Yoga is in the old chapel where all the other ladies dress like her, wearing beads and colours too, and flouncy scarves that fall from them like water. Efa goes there twice a week now, since she met Dafydd, who teaches the class. They use the Sunday school classroom for yoga and other activities, like boxing and karate.

Efa takes me. This week, Efa takes me. And it almost makes up for Pigeon. But I'm too quiet and serious for the ladies at Yoga. And they're jealous of how I'm young and how I can still bend and stretch like a wet bit of willow while they creak and groan like dead wood before you break it. All except for Efa. Efa's like something alive when she does yoga. I'm her sister. Maybe we're proud?

But I can hear them talking about me while they get the blankets out, ready for 'relaxation', where you lie on your back and listen to Dafydd fill your body with feelings.

Efa and her English friend Pam are walking back across the hall with the blankets, one each for them, and one for me.

"She'll come round you know," says Pam, Efa's friend, as if I'm not there. "They always do in the end, take my Henry." Henry is her son who runs the boxing. "I never thought it, never thought he'd do this well, what with all the trouble he'd got into, but *now* look at him!" Efa face doesn't flinch although everyone knows about Henry. He's not exactly a saint.

Dafydd's fiddling with the CD player, trying to find some relaxing music. Pam settles down under her blanket, closing her eyes like Jesus! but a few seconds later she opens one eye again.

"'Course, what you've got to worry about is *drugs*. There's *drugs* everywhere these days, and dealers. She in secondary school now? Yes, well, *drugs,* they get them onto them in the first couple of years, and that's it: hooked! I heard they're taking them before school these days, gets them through the exams they say, but then they get a split personality, like Hannibal Lecter." Pam nods to herself.

The laugh comes up into my nose, and I have to pretend to be coughing. I wish I wish I wish that Pigeon was here. I wish we were here in the chapel again drawing moustaches on all these stupid women who haven't got a clue how serious our lives have got.

Dafydd looks over at us, his heavenly smile breaking briefly, flattening out.

"I'm not worrried about drugs with Iola," says Efa through her teeth.

"FOCUS ON THE BREATH!" says Dafydd, his voice spiralling upwards.

Pam takes a deep snort of an in-breath through her nose.

192

Then mutters, "That's what they all say, honestly! No one thinks it of their own. Take my Henry. He was into all sorts, and look at him now." She closes her eyes, like a satisfied cat.

"Breathe!" says Dafydd.

In, out, in, out, in, out, in.

Relaxation is just more time of thinking about Pigeon. *Pigeon kissed me.* Pigeon told me I killed a man.

36

There's a knocking sound. A hollow knock. It's a beckoning sound. It's the door. Ceri.

She's knocking at the door, so he has to go out. She's not met his mam yet. It isn't a good idea. He can tell. Ceri couldn't handle it, talking to someone who didn't understand and didn't listen. So they go out. He holds her hand. It's like clay, soft and real. They don't have much to say.

Why does she come, he wonders. From her, he gets someone to touch. Someone to want. Someone soft, and like a mother, and like a girl. But she gets just him. He's thin and tough. Like a bad meal. Why does she want him?

"My dad says your mam's sick."

She says it suddenly. They're passing the railings by the park. They've stopped walking, because she said it. It's darkish, so he can't see her face. What does she want him to say? What does she want him to do? He's managed to keep her away from the house up til now, away from his mam. How can he explain to Ceri what's wrong with his mother? Where's the beginning of the story? Pigeon looks for it, in his mind, like finding the beginning of a roll of cellotape. He looks, but there's no sign of it. The beginning.

None of the roughnesses of the story he knows promise openings or endings. And anyway, if he were to start unsticking all this by talking, who knows what story he'd tell Ceri? Who knows what he might turn his life into by telling her about himself.

So he says nothing. He can feel Ceri thinking. He can feel her thinking next to him as they walk together. She's making stories of him, and he's not having it. Pigeon won't let her make this story hers. He holds his silence tight around him, and although she tries to ask him a couple of things, like "What're you doing on Saturday?" he doesn't answer. He guards his silence just as he was taught to in the Centre, and as he was taught to in the shed. They don't hold hands anymore, just walk along the path, past the park, into the wood, along the river. Ceri doesn't know what she's done, not really. But she'll know it's broken. They say "Bye," at the top of the path and they each go. Ceri's face is as blank as a page. Her eyes are inky.

At home, he sits again with the book. He sits with the book not reading.

It's dark now. He looks out of the window into the black garden. There's the square shape of his shed against the coal sky. There are a few stars. That one's Venus, and you can see Sirius, the brightest star, and the Dog Star, and that's almost all.

Which side of the window is inside?

He thinks it suddenly. Which side is he on? It's a strange thought to have. He's disorientated for a second, doesn't know where he is. It's as if things have come apart, and what things mean has left them, detached. There's just him. And what's he? There are no words in his head that second, not even English ones. He's drifting in space. Then he's in the

195

living room, sitting beside his mam with the book on his lap. He begins to read again.

"Many a night she would stand by the open window, looking up through the dark blue waters where the fishes swam. She could see the moon and the stars; they looked paler but larger down here under the sea."

The room's like cold water around him. The room is underwater, but you can still breathe. He takes a long breath, starts again. "Sometimes a great shadow passed by like a cloud and then she knew that it was either a whale or a ship, with its crew and passengers, that was sailing high above her." Pigeon stops again, looks over at his mam, sitting in the dusky corner, rocking. "None on board could have imagined that she stood in the depths below them and stretched her little white hands up toward the keel of their ship."

A word came into his head, a Welsh word. One for which there's no translation.

It was followed by another word. He'd collected it years ago. Cut it out of one of Efa's newspapers.

Dispossessed.

He said the word. Dispossessed. And again. Dispossessed. It was the shed. It was the gun. It was the Centre.

There were two parts of him. One part that had done it, and was proud, and could take the consequences. One part that was angry, had lost, was in mourning. There was a word for that part of him. Dispossessed.

It was not knowing the words anymore. It was gulping for the words, like a fish out of water, or like a bird submerged.

37

I need to talk, to sew myself back together with words. I leave Efa outside the chapel and go down the path by the river, along the road and through the wood, to meet Cher.

In the old barracks there's Cher sitting. She's sitting so still, Cher. She'd have waited forever.

"Hi, Iola," she says. "What's up?" looking at me like she's trying to read a book.

"Nothing."

"Shall we go up to the quarry then?" Cher asks.

We walk up the dusty road to the quarry, the quarry that's still working, where there are still trucks loading and reversing and a few men who've kept their jobs there. There's a big railing and a sign. DANGER it says, KEEP OUT. We hang over the railing and watch the trucks driving up the road that goes up the slate tips to the top of the mountain. From here you can see down to the lake that's been made of one of the quarry holes. The water's blue green. There's something fluorescent in the water. There's some dead trees sticking out of it, they're bleached white as bone.

"Iola," Cher says then. The way she says it makes me turn to look at her, and when I do, Cher's ragged and empty like old clothes. Cher's thinking about saying something again. Her mouth begins to say it over and over, that small breath in when she's about to speak, and then she stops herself.

"What's up, Cher?" I have a feeling again in my stomach, rising up into my throat. There's something wrong with Cher. I know this feeling from the way things have been with Pigeon and with Efa. And then Cher says it.

"I'm going away," she says.

There's silence. A full stop. And it's the full stop I hear. Just the end.

I look at her, I look at my friend.

"What d'you mean?" I say, although I know.

"I'm going away," Cher says again.

"What're you on about? Where?"

"My sister. She lives in Manchester. I'm going to Manchester. I'm going to live with her."

"You don't have a sister."

Cher just stands there, nodding.

"What's her name?"

"Martha."

"Martha?"

"Yes."

I sit down.

"You can't go."

But Cher just nods again.

"Where does she live?"

"Manchester." Cher says it again, and she starts to smile.

I'm up then. "Cher, you can't go." It's my voice, shouting. "You can't Cher, you can't."

But Cher's poking the ground with a stick, and nodding slowly.

Cher's going. Inside everything's closing up. Everything's

closed and aching. I'm like one of Pigeon's mam's dresses, with the hems all closed so that nothing can get out. Around me there's the grey hill, empty and lonely, with the makebelieve shut away.

My insides hurt. My mind is trying to move in my head, and do something with the thought. Cher. Leaving. But all there is, is that long ache, the quarry, the lake below us, the dead trees.

I run. I run up the path through the wet leaves and dirt, Cher calling behind me. Cher running behind. Hot, suffocating tears are doing nothing to stop this, any of it.

It's not until we get to the clearing in the wood that Cher and me slow. Cher gets to me then, breathing heavy and hard. We stop running. We both catch our breath, backs rounded to the clouds, hands on their knees, like when I used to run with Pigeon, for ice creams, back when I'd believe anything.

Cher puts her arms around me. Her arms are warm. They're soft. Cher's body's gentle against me.

Cher pulls away and is looking straight at me.

"I'm glad he's dead, Iola. Glad you did it."

Do I push Cher off? I don't know. I run.

Cher follows me home. She follows me at a distance. I can feel her, and hear her footsteps in the wood behind me.

It's getting dark. The streetlights are on when we get to the road. When I turn there's Cher, plodding along behind as always. We walk, one in front of the other, all the way up the road, lit orange. I'm angry. I don't want to lose Cher, but I don't want to wait for her either.

We walk up the next street, and the next, and to my door, which is a bit open, as always.

I go through the door and Cher follows me in. She doesn't

say anything, just walks in behind me, sits down on the sofa next to Dafydd and begins to watch TV. I ignore her. Dafydd ignores Cher too, as if she's a louse not a girl.

I hate her. Hate her for going. Without Cher there'll be just Pigeon, and I'll be like an apple that's wormed rotten, so that there's nothing, nothing left inside. And it's all of that, those pushing and pulling feelings, hurting and turning it all ugly, that make me get up from the armchair, walk over to the sofa, and do what'll really make Cher hurt.

I give Dafydd a proper woman's kiss on the lips.

Cher's already up and storming for the door, breathing funny as she goes. It's like I've taken all the breath from Cher in that kiss.

Dafydd's standing with his hands gripping my wrists now, like Pigeon did before. He has an expression on his face I've not seen. Almost angry. Almost a smile. Something I don't recognise. And then I know it. Know that he won't stop, not Dafydd, he won't stop for anything.

But he does. It's just that sudden burn of my wrists held tight. His breath. Sour. And the filthy sound of him as we struggle that moment. I kick him in the stomach, and perhaps it's that, cos he gets up and he leaves the room. The room is still full of his breath even when he's gone. And then that's it. Just a kiss. Just a kiss that breaks it all.

On the floor in the living room, a couple of cushions from the sofa, strewn. There's the smell of Efa's breadmaker, making cinnamon loaves. The homey smell. Cinnamon is all wrong. Cinnamon is all wrong. And Cher was right about Dafydd; Pigeon was right again, Pigeon was right.

I walk outside. The street's empty, and it's dark, and on the street, it's bright with stars, like in pictures of heaven.

Just the sound of cars in the distance, like a Welsh R. And it was a kiss. Just a kiss.

I'm outside the shed.

"Cher."

I'm stood outside the shed in the dark.

"Cher."

"Cher."

I'm calling her, and I'm crying. And she won't come out.

"I'm sorry. I'm sorry. Cher. Cher, help me."

"Why did you do that, Iola?" Cher's asking from inside.

"I don't know, I don't know why. Cher, it was me. I did it. I did it," and Cher's looking at me, standing in the door now, and all I can say is, "Cher it was me. I killed Him. Cher it was me."

But Cher just shakes her head. She shakes her head slowly, in that way Cher does when something is too much for her, when she just can't put all the pieces together again, and closes the door.

Later I know Efa's home because I hear the door and hear Dafydd's voice saying, "Hello, Darling. Hello," and Efa and him going quiet. I know they're kissing, and I don't know how Efa bear to.

I *could* tell Efa. "Dafydd kissed me," I should say. But I can't. Because it was me. It was me all along. Later Efa calls me down for supper, and I don't go.

"Dwi'm yn teimlo'n ry dda," I say. And I don't. It's true. I'm not feeling well, and I get into bed, and then Efa comes up, comes into the room, sits on my bed, and strokes my hair. She touches me for the first time in a long while, strokes my hair, my forehead, and she says to get some rest.

Instead I lie and listen to them talking and laughing in my house, downstairs. I can't sleep. I look out the window, at the town below our house. The town looks small and big at the same time. Small and big, like the inside of a balloon, which, when you're in it, is all you can see from horizon to horizon, but when you look at it from the outside, looks like nothing at all.

And I'm angry in a dark, stewing way, angry like a coiled-up spring with it all, but most of all with Efa.

We've told lies, Pigeon and me. I wasn't there, we said, not at Gwyn's house when it was burnt, not at Pigeon's house that night. Pigeon did it all on his own. And me? I did nothing. Nothing. And here I am carrying on like there's nothing wrong. Here I am, when deep down inside there's a black pit, where I'm bad, bad like an apple wormed rotten until there's nothing inside.

It comes over me, like an opening sky. I've got to get away.

38

It'd taken a while before Pigeon knew Cher had left. After a few days of not seeing her he went down the garden to the shed, and her bedcovers and clothes were gone. Pigeon'd thought of running away from that shed himself enough times, so he knew. He went in, sat down on the bare bed, lay back and looked up at the ceiling, that old mobile, no clouds left on it now, only the propeller of the aeroplane and a few bits of string. It was heavier now, the air. This place was emptier, colder. You wouldn't have thought she had mattered. But she did.

After Cher, his mam was quiet and sad, lonely. She sat, looking out of the window, hummed to herself, or just shook her head, silently. Perhaps she'd loved Cher, his mam?

He'd got to the end of it, the story in the blue book, and it was useless. It didn't make sense. There was a bit in the middle where they cut off the mermaid's tongue so she could go to dry land, and that made sense, he could relate to that. But the ending, it was all full of the idea of being good, and believing in God, and so it wasn't for him. It wasn't for him. It was for a little boy with a proper Mam and a Dad who existed for real, a boy who had someone reading him the story in a velvet voice, kissing him goodnight, and leaving him to sleep. It was an old-fashioned story, for a nice little boy. At the end of the story there it was. The lesson. Children like that had to be good for their parents said the story. It wasn't for Pigeon. It wasn't for him.

He'd liked it, the thought of being under the sea, here in his house, with the ghostly world moving above him at the surface. But the story that came afterwards, of princes and princesses and marriage and heaven and angels, and parents tucking you in. He hated that. He hated it.

That was the trouble, a story had to have an ending, and Pigeon didn't do that, endings. Or not then. Pigeon never did them. He was all twists and getting out of it and never coming to the end.

Mam was the same. That was one thing you could say for sure they shared. She never got to the end either, just went round the same cycle, rocking, singing, sewing, rocking, singing, sewing. Pigeon didn't speak to her anymore about his life. He'd read her the story, from the book, but it was like she didn't like it either, because after the first bit, she began to cough, and the cough got worse and worse as it went on, until at the end, he had to stop, get her a glass of water. There was a word for that. Distressed. It was a horrible word. It was a word they used in stories for pretty girls called maidens. But when he thought it about his mam it became an ugly, cruel word. Distressed. Distressed.

And that's how Pigeon felt now too. He felt like that.

Pigeon wasn't going to school or college, Pigeon had no work.

"He can't be left at home doing nothing," the probation man said. So they made him go on this course. It was a taster day they said. If he enjoyed it he might go on a longer course.

They'd finally listened to him. The course was about walls. Stone walls. It was for those walls that made seams all over the mountains, and between all the fields. They told him he'd to be there at nine on the Monday. Pigeon had "Nine on the Monday" in his head; it felt right.

The first day, the teacher was late. Pigeon and the other lads on the course were standing in the yard outside the community centre waiting.

"Fuck this shite," said one of the guys and kicked at the floor. He had an earring, thought he was tough, but Pigeon thought different. Nobody here scared him now, not after Neil at the centre and all that.

"Di o'm yn ffwcin dwad," said the guy again.

But then an old landrover came up the road, and into the yard, and a man started getting out with his dog. The man's hair was white. He walked with a limp across the car park. He wore blue overalls and big boots. The dog was a sheepdog. Black and white and shining. The dog ran straight up to the lads. It ran to the one with the earring, but then, since he pushed it away, it ran to Pigeon.

"Hey," said Pigeon gently. "Hey," he said then. "Hey," and stroked the dog behind the ears.

The man got out of the landrover, came over to them. He looked at Pigeon.

"Elfyn," he said. That was his name. "Nel 'di hi," he said, motioning to the dog.

Nel was sat at Pigeon's feet now. Her body leant against his legs, and she was looking up at him. Pigeon grinned down at her. She was alright, Nel.

"Be di d'enw di 'ta machgen i?" the man asked him then. Why did he ask just Pigeon? Why was he speaking to Pigeon directly and not to the others?

"I'm Pigeon," Pigeon answered. He looked up at the man. Elfyn's eyes were grey. They were small. There were wrinkles in waves around them. His eyes were half-smiling. There was a look in his eyes that knew things.

"That's a good name, lad," he said in Welsh.

"It's my real name," said Pigeon, in English.

"Oh, I don't doubt," the man grinned.

After getting all the others' names. The man just said "Reit ta," and started walking round the back of the building, to where there was a field. The lads looked at each other. He hadn't said if they were supposed to follow. They looked at each other and then slowly started moving after the man.

Pigeon walked across the tarmac after this man and his dog. There was something about him. He wasn't about words. That was good. Pigeon felt good.

In the field round the back there was a big heap of stones. The man was looking through the pile. He didn't even look up when the group got to him. Just kept on looking. Sometimes he'd pick up a stone, or manoeuvre one out of the pile with his booted foot. Then he'd say "Na... Na..." to himself, put it down. Pigeon watched the man. This was interesting.

The other lads started to talk to each other. They were talking as if they had nothing to learn from the man. They talked about last Saturday night. They'd been to town. There'd been a girl who was up for it. Pigeon tried not to hear what they said about her. He was embarrassed for the man and for them, because this wasn't the kind of conversation you had in front of a teacher, not an old teacher like this man. The man just acted as if the conversation wasn't happening.

The man had found some stones he was happy with. He started lining them up on the ground next to each other. The others had stopped watching completely, and they were fooling around now, looking at some pictures in a magazine one of them had brought in his coat pocket. Pigeon kept watching the man. Pigeon looked at the stones. Each one was different. They were like a jigsaw puzzle. Some of the shapes were meant to be together, others weren't. He looked at the stones, and he started to see surfaces and edges. He started to read them in a different way now. Pigeon felt good.

It went on for about half an hour. The man ignoring the lads, the lads ignoring the man. The man had begun to make a wall. You could see it was going to be a wall now. It was going to be two thin walls propped against each other to make a strong stone wall.

"Not being funny mate," said one of the lads finally "but aren't you supposed to be teaching us?"

The man looked up. He half smiled.

After an hour, there was only Pigeon stood there, watching. The other lads had gone to stand in the doorway of the centre, where it was more sheltered. They had to wait around until twelve, to keep probation happy.

Pigeon watched the man. He only chose the flat stones at first. You had to make the stones fit together. The man didn't make anyone learn, but if you wanted to, you could.

When twelve o clock came, the others just wafted off, across the carpark and into town. Pigeon felt a bit awkward then, standing there watching, past the end of the lesson. Maybe he'd better leave now? But hadn't he better say thanks or bye or something? He stood there for maybe ten minutes, watching the man. He'd made a segment of wall now. It looked good, solid. Out of that pile of stones he'd made something that made sense. It was perfect, and not perfect too. Pigeon didn't want to leave.

"Gei di helpu, os 'sgen ti awydd?" the man says to him now. He looks up at Pigeon for a second. There's no trick in the look.

Pigeon considers. He looks at the pile of stones. There's one here. It has a flatish front and back, but a wave down the bottom, and a small chink taken out of the top. It's a simple shape, the kind of shape he's seen the man choose. He should be able to find some other stones to match it.

"Iawn," says Pigeon, like moving his stuff back from the shed to the house. He starts looking through the pile. Picking. Choosing. Making sense of it.

And that's how it begins, with Elfyn, the building things back again, the putting the pieces back in their place.

39

I need to start making money to leave, so I ask Efa if she can get me a job in The Home. She doesn't see why not. But "It's not nice work, you know, Iola," she says, frowning.

"I know. I want a job anyway. Can you get me one?"

"I maybe could; they're always looking for kids like you to do the bad shifts," she says. "They won't pay you much. Why d'you want it anyway?"

"To save up," I say. I don't tell her why. She looks at me a long while.

"It's not such a bad idea," she says, slowly.

On my first day at The Home, Efa walks me there. She walks me up to the door, like she used to at chapel, and then looks at the door, with that same dread, and leaves me to go in on my own. Her turned back is cold. A rejection.

I ring the bell, but no one comes. I ring again, no one answers. Is this what visitors have to do? Stand here on the step in the cold, waiting so someone lets them in to see their old Mum or Auntie? I ring the bell one more time, and then try the handle.

It turns. The door clicks open. The porch is small. There

are some plastic flowers, a visitors' book. But I'm not a visitor, I'm staff. A worker. I open the heavy inner door. There's a young man with tattoos up his arms, vacuuming the blue carpet. He goes into one of the rooms with his whirring hoover, doesn't even look up at me, as if it doesn't matter who it is that has walked in off the street.

I walk into the hall, and stand in the middle for a second. One of the rooms has its door wide open, and there's an old man in there, in just his underpants and a shirt, socks. His back is curved like a swan's neck. He's stood in front of his window, looking out, lost. I think of closing the door, so whoever comes in next doesn't see his bare legs. I don't close the door. I take a step or two further into the hallway.

A lady comes out of the room next door, talking on her mobile phone.

"Yeah, yeah. So I said to him, I don't want to. Don't want to get involved. Yeah. Cos I've got enough on my plate right now, I said. I got enough going on. Know what I mean? Between this place, and the kids and Mam and that. I got enough." She breaks off to say to me, "Be with you in a minute," and then "Anyway," she says into the phone again, "look I've got to go, this girl's here, it's her first day. Alright yep, I'll give you a call. No. No. Yep. Bye then, see you."

She puts her phone back in her pocket.

"Siân," she says.

"Iola."

"Right then. You can come help me with the toilet round."

And that's all. We go together down the corridor, and start at the bottom, working our way up. It's difficult with the old people, toileting them. You have to lift some of them, and some don't want their clothes pulled down, and some want you to stay in the room, and others want you to leave but you can't in case they fall. Toileting takes an hour and a half altogether. One after the other. It's all gloves on, gloves off, wipe, clean, pull up clothes, wheel in, wheel out. One after the other. One after the other. None of the old people talk.

Siân does though, to me.

"So've you got a boyfriend?" she asks, letting an old woman called Meri onto the pan.

Meri slouches to the side, whimpers, and me and Siân have to get her straight again.

"So?" asks Siân.

"No."

"No one interested?"

I can think of two who are, in a kind of way. But it isn't right, the way either of them are interested. Pigeon nor Dafydd.

I'm quiet, and Siân's getting fed up with it, the toileting, you can tell, she'll take it out on the old people, moving them too quick and harsh, telling them to hurry up.

Efa'd said. She'd said watch out for Siân. "She isn't the boss, but she wants to be, and she can get you hired and fired in two shakes."

After toileting, it's lunchtime, and then time for more toileting before tea, and then some people need baths before supper.

And that's the way it goes. You go from one to the other. I don't get told their names. Siân will sometimes say a name, and she does seem to know them, although why she needs to, I don't know, Siân isn't after a conversation.

It's a bad place The Home. You go home tired, and feeling like things have hard edges, like things are meant to hurt you. I want out of it. But I'm saving. I save and wait. Until I'm old enough to leave.

I don't have a proper conversation with any of them until the one with Huw. Huw, the man who'd stood alone in front of the window on my first day here. You can tell even now, looking at him, that he used to be tall. His bones are big. His hands, when you put them on the handles in the bathroom, are heavy and big too. But the fingers don't clasp well any more. You can tell from his look that he's from the quarry. His eyes have that slate look. He's mostly silent.

Siân and me've gone in to him to dress him. The room's dark. No one's drawn the curtains yet. Huw can't get up by himself, his legs don't swing round the bed anymore, and without the frame, which they've left on purpose too far away, he can't lever his heavy bones out of the small single bed.

Siân doesn't say anything, just goes to the window and pulls open the curtains. Huw turns on his bed. There's the sound of angry breathing.

"Reit ta," says Siân, to no one in particular. "Huw!" She almost shouts his name to wake him.

He tries to turn on the bed.

I feel bad for him. Who wants to be woken like this? By someone else and their routine for toilets and breakfasts?

But then Huw's eyes, his grey eyes, are open. He looks at me.

"Wyres Leusa da chi ynde?" he says, as clear as day. *You're Leusa's Granddaughter aren't you?* "Yes," he smiles to himself "Leusa and Ned's granddaughter."

Leusa is Nain. But "Ned?" I'm staring at him.

"C'mon Iola," says Siân. "Lets get him up and dressed."

I'm almost shaking as I take Huw's arm, and help him lever up into a sitting position. He's heavy, and I have to watch my back, which twinges more and more, like Efa's does, ever since I've worked here.

"Ned?" I ask him again.

"Your grandfather." He says it so simply. So simply. The name sinks into me. Ned. Ned my taid, who had another story. Maybe this man knows. Maybe he knows. That old hunger for a real story's back. For a story at all.

"Did you know him? Ned?"

There's a long silence. Maybe I've lost him. Maybe this Huw's gone back into that dreamworld they go to, which must be better than this place.

"We were best mates." He half smiles again. "Yep. My best mate." But then Huw's too busy to talk what with trying to stand, and deal with Siân's hasty, snatching hands as she pulls his clothes on, as if she's packing shopping into bags not caring for an old man who was once my grandfather's best mate. It's not until me and Siân are on either side of him, supporting him, or forcing him to his feet, guiding or cajoling his hands around the bar of his frame, that Huw goes on.

"He wasn't a bad man you know," he says. He looks at me. His eyes are solid.

I bite my lip. In my head there's Nain protesting. *Not a bad man? Not a bad man?* This Huw'd be no match for her.

But Nain's not there to fight this now and so Huw's words are shifting things around.

"Na," says Huw. He smiles, and he puts his hand over mine on the frame. His hand is heavy, suprisingly firm. "He went to Spain, Ned. Volunteered. Brave, that was." Huw's shaking his head now. "Fought the fascist bastards," he says. Then he goes quiet, and just looks at me. "He didn't know Leusa was pregnant." He shakes his head. "He was a brave man, Ned."

It's too much. I step away, Nain's anger making my movements too sharp. It's all Siân can do to hold the old man on his feet. She swears at me.

"What the bloody hell're you doing, you stupid cow," she says.

"Sorry, sorry," I say. "I went a bit dizzy."

"Well come on, help me get this one to the loo. We've got five more to get up before coffee."

Nain's anger subsides. The three of us shuffle across the hallway together. Huw doesn't speak again. He goes into his shell. Into somewhere behind his cataracts, where my taid is.

40

Efa's out when I get home from work, so I can search through Nain's papers properly. I want to know it, want to know what's happened to us, our family on this hill, what's always been happening to us, what's wrong.

There are three shoeboxes of Nain's. All full of paper. The first is just snippets from newspapers. Bits of awful poems and letters she'd had published for a fiver, and competitions or prize draws she'd meant to enter. In the second is all bills and bank statements, most of the bills are overdue and most of the bank statements show how much she owed. In the third box there's her letters, and it's under a heap of Christmas cards I find it, the photo. Men from the quarry stood there, and the women. It's for the Eisteddfod, a choir or a party of singers at least standing to have their photograph taken before they perform. At the front is Nain, I can tell by her eyes, but Nain's young in the photograph, and her face is open, open and fresh and lovely, so that you can't believe she's the same person at all. And then there's a face torn out, and that's Taid. I know because I can feel Nain's fingers all frantic as they tear through the photograph. I can feel Nain in the attic hating him, and maybe more than hate, something worse, more

215

painful. I hold the photograph and I can feel her, hating. More than Efa hates her now even.

I can't see the face, but I can see the shoulders, strong, and he's tall, and you can see a bit of black hair, so Taid was dark. He's in old trousers and a shirt, and isn't dressed as smart as the other men, who're in their Sunday clothes.

That's all of him I find except these postcards, and this letter. It's been scrunched up tight. I can feel Nain's fingers trying to stop me opening it. I can feel Nain's fingers and all her anger holding it crumpled up like this, like a dead bud.

It says a lot of words, all in posh English. It says, *I, Ned Thomas, have decided to give my life to fight an unjust enemy.* And then, in the margin, in Welsh, scribbled: *Leusa, I'm sorry. I'm sorry if I've died in Spain.*

How Nain hated it, Spain. Nain thought everywhere was better than here, than the hill, everywhere except Spain.

I think it: that he must've had a good reason after all. Taid must've had a good reason for all of this.

I can't quite read his joined-up writing. I can't quite read it, but it says "cariad" at the bottom, and he must've loved her, Nain, and he must've had a reason. Like Dad, who must've had a reason for being sick. I hold the letter, I read it over and over. Over and over. I look again at the envelope. It says Barcelona. *Barcelona.*

I hear Huw saying it. *Brave, he was. Fought the fascist bastards.* I don't know about history, but I do know that my taid, even if he was on the wrong side of Nain, he was on the right side of something. *A good man.* Huw says it again with a half smile.

I'm between Huw and Nain.

"Ma'r lle ma'n hanner marw," Nain'd say. *This place is half dead.* But really it was Nain. That was why Dad went too.

Because he couldn't bear Nain being only half a person, and that half being like a dried fig and as empty as chapel.

"There's nothing here for you y'know," Nain'd say, and maybe she's right. Maybe I should leave too. Maybe like Nain said, there's nothing here, nothing left. But what if what's left is everything?

"What're you doing?" It's Dafydd stood in the doorway to Efa's room. He's smiling.

"Get out," I say in a quiet, sprung voice. "Get out."

He stands, looking at me, still half smiling.

"Get out, Dafydd," and then, "I'll tell my sister."

"What will you tell her, Iola? Eh?" he laughs without moving his still eyes. "Anyway I know about you, Iola. I know it was you."

I look away. "Get out," I say. I don't look at him.

"You killed that man didn't you?"

He grins, and he walks towards me. "Pigeon's mother told me," he says.

I almost consider it, what Dafydd wants. The bargain he's trying to strike. They'll make me bad, Dafydd and Pigeon. Like Nain made Taid. Nain made Taid out to be such an ugly, bad thing. Such an ugly person. And soon I'll be like Taid. I'll be just what people decide to say I am. Then my mind does what it did that day with Him. It searches for a way out. Like smoke in a burning house. I lunge past Dafydd, half running half falling down the wooden stairs, grabbing my purse and my earnings off the counter, and out.

41

It bothered Gwyn, the lie he'd told. It bothered him late at night and early in the morning when he lay in his three-quarter-sized bed in his new flat on the quay.

Miscarriage of justice, he thought, rather grandly. Miscarriage of justice!

And he, Gwyn, was a part of it. A small but crucial part. He was the one person who knew. It was like being at the centre of a newspaper story, or the plot of a novel. Except that he was Gwyn. He was only Gwyn. How could he be crucial to anything? Imagine! Gwyn: the piece that held the story in place.

Gwyn squirmed under the pressure, lying in bed, sweating. He squirmed and he squirmed. And then, because it was unbearable, he resolved to tell.

The person he chose to tell was Maggie. Maggie with the brown hair from a bottle. Maggie who knew more about sex than Gwyn had ever dreamed. Maggie who had big unruly breasts, a foul tongue, and who Gwyn had, tentatively, started to think of as His Girl.

"Fuck!" she said now, propping herself up on one elbow in his bed, her heavy boobs indignant against the room.

And then she asked the question that would haunt him:

"What the fuck are you going to do about it?"

There was a terrible imperative to the question. It closed around Gwyn with its expectation. With that question, Maggie took away the freedom of his second stab at childhood. The question made him eat a whole bar of milk chocolate, and made him, instantly, be at Maggie's beck and call.

She marched him down to the police station as soon as they'd finished a good breakfast of bacon and eggs.

Maggie burst through the pinging door, and strode straight up to the counter.

"Miscarriage of Justice!" she said, breathlessly "Miscarriage-of-justice."

Gwyn was pale, standing behind her. He tried to turn back to beige. But all that bacon, all that sex, all that Maggie, had saturated his colours so that he stood out like an ice-cream van in the winter.

The policeman behind the desk, raised an eyebrow.

"Want to make a statement?" she asked.

"Yes! Fuck. Yes," said Maggie.

"Maggie…" said Gwyn.

"Yes, we want to make a fucking statement," said Maggie again.

"No need to swear, madam," said the policeman

"I didn't!" said Maggie her eyebrows climbing.

"Maggie…" said Gwyn again.

"Right then," said the policeman. "Have a seat, and someone'll be with you shortly."

Maggie dragged Gwyn to sit down.

"Now," she muttered at him tersely. "You have to make sure you get the story right."

"Maggie..." said Gwyn.

"You have to make sure they know exactly how it happened."

"The problem is, Maggie..."

"And that the kid's innocent. He's as innocent as Jesus, and that little girl she's a ... she's a..."

"Teenager now," said Gwyn.

"Here," said Maggie, producing a pen, "write down what you're going to say."

She sat, looking over his shoulder as he wrote.

Eight years ago a boy was convicted for a crime...

The door to the office opened.

"Come through," said a young, female policewoman. She looked at them both. "Just one of you at a time," she said.

Maggie looked crestfallen.

"You can make a statement later," the woman said to her.

"It's alright," said Maggie "I've got nothing to fucking say anyway."

Gwyn was led through into the interview room.

"So," said the woman. "What exactly is this about?"

"I'm not really sure," said Gwyn.

"You'll need to be a bit more specific," she said laughing. She was pretty. She had blonde hair. A uniform. "It's about a couple of kids who..." Gwyn stopped.

The woman looked at him. She looked at him long and hard.

Gwyn thought of him, Pigeon, when he was just a boy. That look of pride on his face in the tribunal, standing there, in the glass box, surrounded by adults, as he said the words. *I did it. I killed him.*

Could you take that away from the boy and leave him still standing?

"It's nothing," said Gwyn "I'm sorry. Just kid's stuff. I'm wasting your time."

Outside, Maggie couldn't fucking believe it. She couldn't fucking believe her ears. She went off down the street in a fucking bad temper, and Gwyn, he felt once again a palpable, relief at being rid of another Hell of A Woman, at least for the rest of the afternoon.

42

Pigeon goes out with Elfyn every day. They go round building walls for people. Pigeon's getting better at it, choosing the right stone for the right place, fitting them all together.

They don't speak much, except to Nel, the frank-eyed collie, who watches them all day, sniffs around the stones, and comes to lean against Pigeon's legs, scavenging for comfort, to be stroked.

"Dyna ti," Pigeon says to her. "Gw' gel."

The Welsh has come back a bit, at least when he's outside with Elfyn, when they're doing the walls. It feels right then. But still, with his mam, or with anyone else, there's no words, just a blank space in his mouth. A space that's bright, too bright, so that when he tries, his mouth's just empty, or perhaps not empty, too full, like when you try to speak with a mouth full of white bread.

They sit to have lunch, Pigeon and Elfyn, leaning their backs against the wall they've made, unwrapping the sandwiches Elfyn's brought them, unrolling them from the brown paper. They're big, thick sandwiches. They taste like something real. The cheese in them is tangy and spicy and good. Half the sandwiches are for Pigeon, and half for Elfyn. They don't speak as they eat.

But after eating, as they drink bitter black tea from Elfyn's big flask, there'll be a conversation.

"Chei di'm gwell na'r mynyddoedd 'ma." Elfyn says today, looking past the wall at the hills.

"Na," Pigeon agrees.

"Does na'm gwell lle yn y byd." Elfyn says it quietly, because it's a fact.

Pigeon smiles. And right now it's true. They're on top of it, on top of the world on this heap of a hill by this wall, and there's nowhere better, nowhere better. There's nowhere else in the world.

His mam's worse and worse. She sits. She stares into space and she drinks.

"Ti'n yfed Pigeon?" Elfyn asks one day. *Do you drink, Pigeon?*

"Na," says Pigeon.

"Na fina machgen i. Na finna. Hen beth gwael 'di alcohol. Difetha bywyda' a Difetha pobl," says Elfyn.

Pigeon sits quietly, knowing Elfyn's right. Alcohol is a home-wrecker, a people-wrecker a medicine with terrible side-effects.

Elfyn looks at him. Then gently. "Sut ma' dy fam, Pigeon? Ro'n i'n i nabod hi, blynyddoedd yn ôl 'sdi. Pan o'dd ei theulu hi'n cadw'r post."

Elfyn? Knew his mam once? There it is again, like her name, Mari, as if she was once someone real. It's the gentlest of invitations. Between the words there's Elfyn beckoning. *You can talk to me. You can talk to me my lad.* That's what's between the words.

"Mam's OK," says Pigeon. Keeps putting up walls.

And that's it. The moment's passed. Elfyn knows better than to invite more than once.

So Pigeon learnt to build walls. He built them the old way, with local rock, granite and slate. Pigeon hardly spoke now. But he was alright. That's what they said. "Quiet, but alright."

"He does a good job with the walls, and you can trust him, at least with that," was what they said.

And the people who wanted the walls, they couldn't care less about the whispers.

All around him, the town whispers. And Pigeon comes to depend on the whispers in the town. They tell Pigeon a story that he needs. The story of what Pigeon did to Him that night on the hill.

Perhaps he got off lightly, in a way, Pigeon. Just a short sentence, relatively speaking, and then a couple of years on parole. What he lost, when he gave in to his own stories, perhaps wasn't so great, just a few words, or, to be precise, a home's worth. And only Elfyn sees the marks left by the words, the faint imprint of having been once a part of something, only Elfyn can coax Pigeon to come a little closer to home, to utter a few sparse words of Welsh.

The old man greets each one as if it's made of gold, or purple slate.

It's with Elfyn, doing the walls, month after month, Pigeon'll think.

Home, the hill, has a long memory, and it knows the story of what happened to Pigeon, and what he did. People whisper when he passes. People may whisper. But they're only words. And he doesn't care. Doesn't care for words anymore. He barely speaks. And he never speaks his own language anymore. It belongs to a different time, a different boy, with shoulders delicate as eggshells. This Pigeon has only one story.

Killing Him had Pigeon back in the middle of it all. It had

done what none of the words could. That he'd managed it held him together, almost.

But thinking about Iola made him uneasy. Even now, years after it all, there was an uncomfortable feeling, of things not quite sitting right, not quite being ready to be put to rest.

There was a kind of peace he was after. He wanted it all settled. He wanted it to be simple. There was something understandable in the formula he'd made: Crime, punishment, rehabilitation. It matched the formula he'd made for Him: abuse, anger, retribution. But Iola. She didn't quite fit the pattern. She stuck out of his life in a way that didn't sit right with him.

Iola was interrupting his train of thought all the time. There was a kind of a gap, a missing link he couldn't ignore. She was a headache. He couldn't see her clearly. What did she look like? What did she sound like? What did she have to say for herself? He couldn't think. When he did remember times he'd spent with her, she was always listening, taking in, watching. What had she been thinking, Iola? What had she been thinking all that time?

She was caught up with it all. You couldn't avoid it. She was caught up with it all, with the words that were locked away in his head and wouldn't properly come back. She was there, in his head. No amount of time could get her out of that white, cold place in his head where the words were. That wasn't a good place for her to be. It'd make her sick.

Elfyn gave him half a sandwich.

"Diolch." he said. And Elfyn nodded, as if that was the most natural thing in the world, Pigeon saying it: "Diolch".

He'd seen enough of it with his Mam. Iola was in trouble. He couldn't get her out of that place in his head, and she wouldn't get that sickness out.

It was when you asked too much of a person, they went into the white space. Even Pigeon could feel it beckoning, that place. His mam never came out of it anymore.

"Ti'm am fyta'r frechdan 'na?" Elfyn was asking. I'll happily eat it if you don't, he adds.

Pigeon looks at the sandwich. He takes a bite. It's tangy and spicy and good.

He'd better talk to her. She's got a piece missing. Like a wall with a stone laid wrong, or missed out. He'd better get her that piece.

He spent the afternoon writing a letter to her in his head. It made sense the letter, but it was in English. It was a nice letter. *It's alright,* it said. *It's alright.*

She would get the letter, and she'd be alright.

They finished that section of the wall early, so he went home an hour ahead of the normal time, walking back along the igam ogam road, with the holey fence, where the bullocks could come through if they wanted to enough.

Today they didn't. The sun was low, and the light from it slanted onto the fields, the brambles, the gorse of the hillside. Pigeon was full of space inside him. Peace it was called, but that was a grand, flimsy word for something so specific and still.

He'd talk to her, and then it'd be alright. Finally it'd be over. Iola would come out of that place in his head, and he'd get the words back, one by one. But he was going in the right direction. He was finally going in the right direction. It was something to do with Elfyn and the walls that'd done it.

He walked into the crooked house through the front door. Lately he'd started doing that. Using the front door. It felt good.

He walked past his mam in the dark living room. He opened

the curtains, went to the kitchen to put the kettle on, grabbed a tea bag from the jar, and another one, for his mam. He stood, watching some birds in the wide sky outside, until the kettle boiled. He poured the water over the bags, stewed them, added milk for his mam, three sugars for him, one for his mam. He carried it through, placed his mam's on the table at her side, picked up a notebook, started the letter.

Iola, he wrote. It's Pigeon. I hope you're alright.

He stopped. Crossed out the last sentence. Sat with the pencil in his hand. Where did you begin untelling a story? He couldn't find the end of it, or the beginning to begin unravelling from.

That man, He was a bastard, he wrote.

The room hardened around him. Something made him look up. He looked at his mam. She was motionless, staring straight ahead. He looked at his mam. Then he knew it. He thought he knew it, silently, somewhere inside. Dead?

But she wasn't. This time she wasn't. She'd taken a pack of pills, but when the ambulance came, screaming up the hill, they woke her with a drip, and inside the ambulance, with Pigeon stroking her hand and whispering I love you I love you, she wound slowly back to life.

They kept her in that night, and Pigeon came back to the house on his own. It was the first time he'd ever been here alone. He slept on the sofa. The house creaked around him, empty. Like a white lie.

43

You can see it, how Pigeon's finding his answers. That's the way it is with him. Telling his own stories, and sticking to them, so that you can't figure out what your story is all about, because it just seems like part of his. I keep at it. Working. Working. I keep on pretending my way through the town. They say I can really go places. *Have you thought about University?* they say. They tell me about places far away with long, exotic names where I might go, if I want to. They show me a prospectus. They think I'd make a good teacher. Efa's keen.

"You could really go places." She repeats it, like they all do.

It makes me feel sick. The thought of leaving Pigeon.

"'ve you ever thought about leaving?" I ask him, sitting on the very edge of his tidy new sofa, afraid to put a foot out of place.

"What d'you mean?"

"You could leave this house, go somewhere else, start fresh?"

He laughs. "I haven't even started here!" he says.

"Pigeon." I feel desperate. "You've got potential." The words sound wrong here. Potential is an understatement for that little boy with the green eyes, who could do anything. But I carry on.

"You're cleverer than I am. You could really *do* stuff." I stop, because he's laughing. He's doubled up, laughing.

When he's finished, and the house straightens, he looks at me, his face going cold again.

"God, Iola. You really don't get it do you?" There's a silence and then, "I need to fix things here. Can't be thinking about going anywhere else can I?"

I think about this. Then I nod. He is fixing it slowly, fixing his house, fixing his mother, fixing his mother tongue.

I think of the story of the 'The Little Mermaid', which Pigeon still keeps in his house, and which I can't bring myself to take back. I remember Efa reading the story, so much more ugly and painful than the Disney version, but so much more real. How the mermaid lost her tongue when she turned against her home in the water, but how, in the end, what she needed was to go back home, beneath the water, find her voice again. Pigeon, he's the same. He just needs to get this house in order, piece by piece, find his way to a home to call his own, and the words and words of him will come slowly to the tip of his tongue.

I buy myself a train ticket. It's easy. You just go to the counter, and ask. I wait, on the narrow platform, for the train. There are people saying goodbye to each other. And people with big suitcases, going somewhere far. I have nothing with me except for some money, and no one to say goodbye to this time. Eventually, the train pokes through the tunnel like an eel, and rolls dead slow into the station.

I'm going to see Dad. I decided it last night. I want to know him. I want to know what he means in his own story, instead of just in ours. I'm going to see the man who packeted the chicken, and wove the statues in the garden out of wire, and left us.

I sit on the train, watching the green, irregular fields passing, and then the towns as they get bigger and bigger on the way out of Wales. No one sits next to me the whole way. At Chester, you have to change. I get off my train and stare at all the screens. There are the names of so many towns going down them, arrival times, departures. Liverpool? Liverpool?

I must have said it aloud because, "It's that one, love," says the guard.

The Liverpool train is ugly. There are bits of chewing gum on the floor, no tables. The seats are old and tattered. But it's only for half an hour. Mostly we go through tunnels and along bits of track between buildings now. Our green and grey hillside feels a long way away. It feels like maybe it doesn't matter as much as I thought.

I don't feel afraid, getting off the train. I have a map. On the map I can see where Dad's house is, the place where he stays now, according to Efa. She gave me the address as soon as I asked.

"I thought you'd want to go one day," she said.

"Have you been there?"

"Once or twice," she said. I had the feeling it was more.

There were so many questions to ask her about Dad, but I didn't know where to begin so I just asked nothing, and she said nothing except, "Be careful".

In Liverpool the buildings are tall and go on and on. Walking along my map, it's just street after street. The trees grow out of the tarmac here, crack it, and push through from the earth below.

This street is Dad's. It has lots of small, brick houses, tiny yards out the front.

The man who opens the door is old. He's stooped like a question mark and has grey hair. He has a white beard, ruckled skin and my eyes. He looks at me.

"Yes?" he says.

I stare at him, and say nothing.

"What do you want?" he asks. And then looks past me up the street, as if I'm no one.

He doesn't know who I am. I look at him a long while. Then, quietly, I say it.

"Iola dwi," I say, "Eich merch."

Inside Dad's house it's pretty dark, and there's bits of metal and wood everywhere, so he's still doing that. I follow him along the corridor to the kitchen. He walks very slowly. The house smells of something I don't recognise. When I see the ashtray, with a long roll up cigarette in it, I know what it is.

Dad makes tea. His hands are shaking.

Every first conversation has to start somehow.

"I didn't think I'd see you again," he says in Welsh. "Efa said you didn't want to know." His Welsh sounds like it hardly gets used, creaky.

"I didn't," I say. I smile.

"You're tall," he says. His voice is a wavering, uncertain note.

"So're you," I say. Neither of us mention our eyes. The same dark, dark blue. Like the bottom of the sea.

"I was. Not so much now. Bent over with bad health," he shrugs. There's a silence. So many questions to ask, but I can't think of the words.

"Efa says you do well at school," he says.

Is that pride in his voice? Is that?

"Not bad," I say. The corners of his mouth twitch just slightly.

He sets a big mug of tea down in front of me. Milk, no sugar. He makes it like that for me without asking. That's how I take it. Milk, no sugar, but he wasn't to know was he?

"I'm s..." he starts, but I interrupt him.

"I killed someone."

He stops, and we stare at each other, me and this man who has no excuses. I have no excuses either. Or perhaps I do?

"When?" The surprise cuts through all the rubbish, the apology I'm not giving him a chance to make because I can't accept it.

"When I was a kid. He was my friend's step-dad. He was nasty."

He looks at me, shocked. Me being here at all. Me confessing.

"He was going to kill my friend, I think. So I killed him, with his own gun." It sounds like a film.

"OK," he says, as if I've just told him I broke a glass. "Does anyone know?"

"One person, maybe two."

"What're they going to do about it?" He leans back in his seat, considering.

"Nothing, I think."

"Does Efa know?"

"No."

"Are you sure?"

"No. Sometimes I think she does. She's never been the same with me, since it happened."

"OK," he says again.

"Tell her?" he says.

There's a long silence. Then he laughs, a low laugh.

"It's good to see you, Iola," he says.

It's good to see him too, even though he's old and hopeless. It's good he has no excuses.

When I tell her, she's sitting in her room in front of the dressing table, brushing her hair.

"I know," she says, without missing a stroke with the hairbrush.

I watch her face. It doesn't flinch. I stand there watching.

"Don't tell anyone will you?" she says to me.

"I already have," I say. "Sort of. I've told Cher. Pigeon's mam knows, and Pigeon."

She puts down the brush. "That's too many people, Iola!"

"And Dafydd," I say quietly.

"Dafydd?" she says.

"Yep. He found out. He threatened to tell you."

"Threatened?"

I nod.

She's looking at me, straight at me.

"He's a nasty piece of work isn't he?" she says.

I nod.

"I saw him with some young girl in town the other day," she says. "All over her, he was." She looks like she's going to cry. But instead, she stands and comes to me, puts her arms around me. Her warm arms.

"Out on his ear, he is," she says quietly, "Out on his ear." And she goes to the record player which has sat there for so many years, waiting to play our music again. She takes out a black disk, sets it on the turntable and places the needle against it. A slow waltz, ghostly like half a memory, but sweet too, like long-lost Sundays, plays into the room, and we begin to dance together. My sister and me. We dance slowly, and I hold onto this rare time when I feel honest and true and safe.

44

When he visits her, Pigeon's mam lies in a cold bed. The bed where the mermaid lies is placed in the centre of the room. There's no indication which end is which. The bed where she lies has no head and no foot. It's disorientating, cold; a bed base, mattress, white cotton sheet. The bed where she lies has no pillow. It's like an altar, and she is the sacrificial lamb. The room (the chamber) is also rectangular. There's nothing on the walls and no other furniture, apart from the bed where she lies. The walls are painted a pale green. The floor is also green, linoleum, of a slightly darker shade. That's it: floor, walls, door, and, in the middle of it, the bed, and the mermaid, lying.

On the ceiling there's a mark. Someone has chipped the paint on the ceiling. How did they do it? It's a high ceiling, and there are no weapons here. Nothing allowed in that could damage, hurt, break. Pigeon looks at the small mark up there on the ceiling and he thinks. But he can't think. The world's full of stale mysteries, even in an empty chamber. Perhaps his mam's a riddle?

The doctor seems to think so. Emanuel, he's called. He has dark skin like the skin of a tree.

"Are you her son?" he asks.

"Yes," says Pigeon.

"Are there any other relatives, anyone to contact?"

"No."

"Any friends?"

"No."

"No friends?"

"None that I want you to contact."

"Right." He sighs.

"When can she leave?"

"Not yet." The doctor turns to Pigeon's mam "Are you hearing voices, Mari?"

"No."

"Good." He ticks something on his chart. "She's responding well to the medication." he says.

"Pigeon?" his mam is looking towards him. Smiling a watery smile.

The doctor starts when she says the name.

"She was calling to Pigeon in her sleep," he says. "It's your name?"

"Yes," says Pigeon. "You know, the grey ugly birds that are everywhere." Pigeon half laughs at himself. Then he stops "The ones that carry messages," he says. "The ones that always find their way home."

The doctor looks blank. He writes a few notes on his clipboard, and leaves them alone. Pigeon wants to run after him, to tell the doctor how his name is a dignified, real name. To tell him about how, in old-fashioned wars, people used pigeons to carry messages of war, and then, if they could find a nice, clean pigeon, unlike himself, not grey, or slate coloured, they used that as a message of peace. Pigeon wants to tell how his name's also the word for a language, a version of someone else's tongue, someone else's story adopted and grown and made into your own until it's better than the original. Pigeon, who collected his own name first, before any of the other words he put under his bed like a hamster making a nest, would like to tell the doctor these things, but he'd balk at telling him, what no one must know, that pigeon is also the word for a victim, which is what people would think Pigeon was, if they ever knew that he'd been punished for something he didn't do.

On the ward there's a small common room, where patients are allowed to go to sit in the dark, grubby chairs, and smoke if they want, or talk. There's a man in there almost all the time. Rich. He has grey hair. He's been in for months he says. Pigeon doesn't ask why. He's quiet enough. Nice. Except sometimes he looks at one place for too long, and then nods at the empty room, and seems to gesture to someone, as if he's agreeing with something they've just said, with their invisible argument. But Rich is clever, and, if he catches one of the staff observing him, he'll halt his arm, change expression, pretend that there's nothing in the room, no one haunting him.

Pigeon spends as much time as he can visiting, hanging around the ward, or in the common room, so that, although he avoids them, the nurses find evidence of him everywhere, scrunched-up pieces of paper, or paper aeroplanes. The nurses tried to keep an eye on him, but found that he had a habit of not being where you thought he was. They'd look for him in the common room and find just a magazine pile tipped to the floor, three magazines open on the blue carpet, as if someone had been lying on their belly, reading the articles, and in the air there was the smell of tobacco, not Rich's dark bitter kind, but the blond, sweet stuff that Pigeon has favoured from age eleven.

His mam sees a psychiatrist, a psychotherapist, an occupational therapist. His mam sees a doctor, several nurses. His mam sees an addiction counsellor. His mam acts as if she sees none of them. This goes on for weeks.

Finally the doctor asks Pigeon what he thinks they should do.

"Make her talk," says Pigeon "Make her talk to you."

So the doctor gives the psychologist two more weeks, and asks her to do some family counselling too. Family counselling is where Pigeon sits with his mam and the counsellor, and the counsellor asks questions which Pigeon answers as briefly as possible, and his mam doesn't answer at all.

But this time, when Pigeon arrives in the pale-coloured room with the coffee table, the three comfortable chairs, the flowers in the pot, the counsellor with her notebook, it's different. His mam, who's been here for a session before he arrived, has been crying. Proper tears. Pigeon looks at her tear-stained face, and feels relief. Some dam must have broken. Some silence.

The counsellor's looking nervous. Why? She's looking at the door, and then back at Pigeon. She's looking at the panic button to her right.

"Pigeon," says the counsellor. "Your mother's been telling me about what happened to Adrian."

Pigeon sits, perfectly still.

"I'm going to have to pass the information on, Pigeon. Do you understand?"

Pigeon nods. He goes to his mother, hugs her, and nods, then he leaves the room.

The policewoman who arrives at the front door is pretty and blonde. Pigeon opens the door, and then tries to close it again in her face. But she sticks a foot out to hold it open.

238

"Alla i gael gair?"

"What about?"

"I wanted to ask you some questions about what happened all those years ago."

It's strange that she's come on her own. The police always come in twos. Pigeon can understand that. He and Iola always went everywhere in a two, back when they had a criminal to catch, evidence to collect, stories to build and break.

"You mean the murder?" asks Pigeon with a grin.

"Yes. That." She smiles grimly.

"Ask away."

"Can I come in maybe?"

It's strange she asks that, when she's on her own.

"I'm a convicted murderer you know," he says, grinning.

"I know," she says. "Can I come in anyway?"

"No," says Pigeon. You don't invite people in when they come to the front door.

"OK," she says. She motions to the bench Pigeon's put out in the little bit of gravel in front of the house. "Can we sit there?"

"OK," says Pigeon, and steps out of the house.

They sit down on the bench. The street has a view down the hill, a view over the town and over other streets, emptied and feather grey. Lately Pigeon's been sitting here, watching it, the town.

"Pigeon," she says. "That's what you like to be called isn't it?"

"That's my name," he says.

"OK," she says "Look. I know you confessed, and you were convicted, but am I right in thinking you didn't do it?"

"What makes you say that?"

"Two people've been to the station."

"Two?"

"I can't tell you who," she shakes her head.

"Gwyn?" says Pigeon straight away.

He can tell by her face that he's right.

"And that woman. The counsellor?"

Right again.

"The thing is," says the policewoman, "There's no evidence your mam's right," then she looks at him, straight into his eyes, "except if you can give me some," she says.

Pigeon looks at her. He thinks of the evidence he hid. The lies he and Iola told. He looks at her.

She says, "My boss doesn't believe it anyway, Pigeon. He thinks it's a waste of time me coming here. But if you can just tell me something, p'rhaps we could get your conviction overturned." She looks at him, with frank, kind eyes. Like a mother. Like a real mother.

Just then three children come along the silver road, two girls and a boy, running, still running in their feral, violent playtimes, laughter bubbling bright and dangerous into the white sky as they jump over the wall at the end of the street, and into the open country beyond. Their language clatters behind them between the gorse and heather, the threatening cattle, and the idiot sheep.

Pigeon thinks of the final meaning of his name, standing there with her. Pigeon is *a case in point*, *a matter,* like the matter of Iola, of Him, of Pigeon's mam and of Pigeon, like the matter of this story, here.

"No," says Pigeon, standing up from the bench "You're wrong," he says.

It was days before he could face the clear-out. First he opened the windows. Let the air in. Let it in to blow out any shadow left by his mother. The breeze that thrust through the open window unsettled the piles of paper, the dust, the grief that lay all over the house. He let it. He let it in. He took a bin bag and started to lift individually the things that were his mother and to thrust them into the black space of the bag. Ashtrays, beer cans, dresses, hangers, needle, thread, old faux jewellery, tights, underwear, handkerchiefs. He spared her nothing, this mother of his that had left him. She could either leave for real now or come back made new. Occasionally, as another part of her was chucked out, a small refrain rang in his head, a ditty or a folksong, some tune she'd learnt in a broken off part of her story. He didn't know where she'd learnt those songs, he'd never met a grandparent, an aunt, an uncle, nothing. They had no family. But in those tunes you got a sense of it. A connection to something. Into the black bag, and they were gone.

Once the bags were filled and taken out to the bins at the end of the street, the cleaning began. Pigeon was meticulous. Every shred of her had to be brushed, mopped, scoured away. She was to have nowhere to hide. No dark, untouched corner where she could sit rocking, humming to herself and ignoring him, ignoring her son, Pigeon.

The house began to straighten out. You could almost see it. Under Pigeon's orders, the bricks began to stand more upright, the roof corrected its angle, things became square again. When it was all done, Pigeon himself took a shower, scrubbing and scrubbing his white skin until it was so clean it squeaked. He stepped out of the shower, his old skin shed. Pigeon, a new thing, dried himself in the long light that flooded in through his clean windows.

When Pigeon saw her standing in his doorway, a small rucksack on her back, it went through him. It was a feeling you couldn't describe, something cold, and hot at the same time. Loss and gratitude and anger and wanting.

He wanted her. He wanted her pale hair and thin, delicate skin. He wanted her narrow shoulders, her half smile. Her guilt. Most of all that was what he wanted. It ran through him occasionally, the idea, that it had been her all along, her stood behind the gun, holding it. But he pushed it back. It had nothing to do with her after all. Couldn't have anything to do with her. She was just a ghost, but a ghost he wanted, he beckoned back and back to him. He wanted her, the ghost Iola, just as you always do want a spectre before it disappears.

She'd come after his mam left him there on his own. Although he'd been alone a long time, the house felt empty when his mam was in hospital.

To the quiet, empty house Iola came. She stood there, in the doorway, crying.

"I'm sorry, Pigeon. Oh God, Pigeon, I'm sorry."

"What for?"

She looked at him. Her red eyes stopped pooling. She sniffed wetly.

"For your mum. For this."

"*She's* not sorry. It's what she wanted isn't it? Mam? To go. Get out of here? Don't bloody cry about it." He walked through into the lounge.

"Aren't you sad?" She sat down on his sofa.

Pigeon thought about it. Is that what you called it. This cold empty hungriness for a mother that had not existed for years.

"No," It couldn't be. Sad was too tame a word.

Hunger. That's what this was. Hunger.

"She'll not come back," he said. "There's no point in crying, Iola. She'll not bloody come back."

It was what he'd learnt early on. There was no point in speaking to his mam if she didn't respond. Didn't answer with a word or a look or a gesture. Better to sit tight with the hunger. Hold the hunger in place with your own silence. His mam never really came home after He moved in.

Iola looked at him.

"Nei *di* ddod adra, Pigeon?" she asked him. Will *you* come home?

He looked at her. He understands the question perfectly. Will he come home? Will he.

"Come with me up the hill, Iola." He said it quickly. He'd to get the words out before they dried from his tongue.

Iola looked surprised, stood here in her nurse's pinny. But she nodded.

On the hill it was boggy today after so much rain. They skirted the field, keeping away from the cattle. A herd of nervy bullocks that had just been put out and were hyperactive and followed them vaguely. Iola just ignored them, and for once Pigeon followed her, copying her long strides. She'd grown tall lately, Iola. Almost as tall as he was. He had it again then. The feeling that she was overtaking him. The feeling that she'd one day leave him. Leave him to this.

At the top of the hill they looked out at it. Their town. Its slow streets. Its shifting houses. The fidgeting gardens where cats trailed across fences, catching their small springtime prey, the poking chimneys, a couple of them smoking, even on a warm day. The town mumbled to itself beneath the deep clouds. Mumbled to itself of killings and games and lies. Even the clouds couldn't muffle its mumbling, even the clouds couldn't entirely smother the life out of this babbling town on the hill.

Pigeon reached for Iola's hand then. And she held his. Her small hand was cool. They sat like that, looking down at their town. He put an arm around her. Her hair smelt good. He kissed her hair.

She didn't move until he was ready, ready to walk the steep slope back, past the cattle stood against the hedgerow expecting rain, back along the snaking path, to the home he was making.

But he didn't go home, not yet. First he led Iola to the quarry, toward what had been hidden there so long.

45

I walk behind Pigeon. Along the road that leads up to the slate tips, small grey and white houses stick from the fog, from the bald hills, like squint teeth. It's raining lightly. The tarmac shines like a black ribbon ahead of us and slate gravestones glint wet in the churchyard as we walk past. How many of those men here had been buried first by the quarries, in the belly of the cut-away mountain? Looking toward the heaps of the slate tips that glint and flicker, wet and shining in the pale sunlight, you can't help thinking of them, those men, the men that were here when Nain was young. The men like the man that left her.

Pigeon turns at the top of the road, in the middle of all this nothing and cloud. I follow him. He goes through the gate to the quarry. It clunks behind him. He ignores the yellow danger signs and barbed wire as usual, clambers under the barrier, and goes towards it, the clearing between the tips where we used to throw stones into the pool of the old quarry below. I follow him as usual.

We're in the middle of the empty quarry, and all this beautiful deadness. Pigeon has stopped, and is standing, as if he's listening. Perfectly still. Waiting.

"Why here?" I ask him. I try to smile. But it's not a certain smile. Nervous.

"Why not."

"Before you say anything. There's something I want to say."

"Don't Iola. Don't." His English words are bare and useless.

"I wanted to say sorry." My English words are so tiny and vast.

"What for. It wasn't your fault He died."

"No?"

"No."

"Whose fault was it then?"

"His."

"*He's* dead."

"Yep."

We're quiet a bit.

"D'you mind that He died?"

"Why would I mind?" Pigeon gives a dry laugh.

"It was the gun that did it."

I hear myself say it, and I don't know why I did.

46

Pigeon had never considered it before. Perhaps she was right. Maybe it was the gun. That small gun they'd showed him again, in the white room, asked him if that was the kind of gun he'd used. They'd never found it, the real one.

"Yes," he'd answered them.

"Show us how to shoot it."

"Here?"

"Yes."

"What d'you want me to shoot?"

"That wall."

"The wall?"

They nodded.

"OK," he said.

He'd taken the safety catch off. Click. Held it in his hands, two hands, he knew how it could throw a person to the ground. He could feel them watching him in this small room he couldn't get out of where what you'd done was all that you were. He pointed the gun at the wall. It was like an animal in his white hands. His hands were shaking. That was the animal, the dog, growling. It snarled in his hands, and all he could do was stand while the dog did it. The dog bit at the wall, the box, this pigeonhole.

But it had no bite. He had no bite left. They'd taken out the bullets.

He walks away from Iola, up into the quarry, beckons for her to follow him. She does, obediently, like she did when they were kids.

Pigeon goes uphill, to a tunnel that's cut through the mountain for the quarry. There are small rails in the tunnel floor, used to cart slate from one part of the quarry to the other and take it down and all over to make the perfect, clean roof slates that shelter everyone else from this rain. Pigeon follows the railed tunnel into the dark. A chink of light at the end of it shines green, and he scuffs towards it, Iola behind him, as she always used to be. At the end, the tunnel opens like a lily, opens into green, ferns and moss and caught sunlight. *Awstralia* people call it, this quarry hole, this lost world. Awstralia's black, and slate blue, and luminescent green with ferns. In Awstralia there's the steady seep of rain falling through the mountain, through heather and gorse and earth and stone and slate and bedrock, drip, onto the dark slate.

Pigeon kneels on the ground beside a slit in the slate wall of the quarry, a narrow shaft not completely blasted. He puts his arm into the split. Grappling around. Looking for something there.

"What…" Iola starts asking, and then sees the brown package he's pulling from the rocks, its old brown paper and brown tape crumbling around the hardness of what's inside. Iola stares at it. She stares at it. Pigeon hands the package over.

"It's yours," he says. "Open it."

"Pigeon. No."

"Well *I* will then," and he takes the package back. He begins to pick and tear at the tape. It comes off without resistance, almost crumbles away, like lies can, leaving what's underneath, black and festering and cold.

The gun.

Pigeon watches her, looking at it. She's waiting, waiting for some feeling to pass.

"It's smaller than I remember," she says.

He passes it to her.

"It's colder than I remember," she says quietly as she takes it in her two hands.

47

What comes into my head, as I hold the gun, is just fear. Is just whiteness, and pressure. I stand holding it, looking at Pigeon and then this:

There's a light in the crooked house. I don't want to see Him so I go past the house, and down the garden towards the shed, and that's when they make sense, the noises. And that's when I know. I know what they are. I'm not stupid. I can hear Him shouting. And I can hear the sound of hitting. But most of all I can hear Pigeon. And maybe it's that. Maybe it's that, that crying that's like a kid, Pigeon, who I love, I love, crying like he's just a kid, that makes me know I have to get in the way of Him just so He stops. I'll make it happen myself.

I'm so quiet, and I move so carefully, it's like I'm not me. I'm not Iola. I'm someone better. Someone who knows exactly what to do. She's strong and careful and she moves up to the house, pushes open the door, hears His shouts, the sound of Pigeon crying, and then quiet. The room and what I'm seeing begins to make a picture.

There's Pigeon standing in the room, and there's Him holding Pigeon to the floor, and then I see it, Pigeon's holding it to His head.

In the crooked house, He sees me. He moves. And He's knocked it from Pigeon's hand and it's gone in the air, and then across the floor until it's right by my foot. It's like something that isn't real, sitting there, by my foot. And He doesn't care that I'm here, that I've got in the wrong story, He doesn't care; He's got Pigeon by the neck like a bird. Like Nain wringing the neck of a bird.

I know what I'm supposed to do. Something big. And I move so perfectly. So perfectly. I get it from the floor, and I lift it. I lift it. And I stand with it in my hand. It's like something that isn't real in my hand. He's ignoring me. Focusing on what he's killing. He holds Pigeon down by the throat, and Pigeon is changing colour. And I hold it. It's heavy. It's not like something real. I wait until Pigeon looks at me. Until he sees me, sees how I'm in on it this time, well in. Then holding it while it shoots is like holding an animal that's too strong, holding a dog while it bites someone deep.

It was it, it was it. I didn't think it would happen. Not in a real way. And I'm on the ground, and I'm hurt, because the sound and it were stronger than me. I'm on the ground. And He's lying on top of Pigeon.

And then Pigeon has pushed Him away. Pigeon's face is white. Pigeon's face is bone white and he doesn't speak. There's the sound of his mam singing. She's still rocking. She's still singing. Pigeon and me are staring at Him forever.

"Dos adra, Iola," says Pigeon after an empty time. Pigeon's still not looking at me, still staring at Him on the ground. Go home, Iola, he says, taking it from my hand. Go home. Don't tell anyone. Don't even tell Efa. Act like this is nothing to do with you. Go home, Iola. Home.

So I follow him again, Pigeon, follow what he says. Go home, go home, over the fence, along the path by the river. Go home and don't say anything, don't ever say anything.

And even now it makes no sense, no sense that Pigeon'd take the blame. Except perhaps he wished it was him. Wished it was. When I turned and looked back at the house, I remember now how Pigeon was standing looking down at Him, lying with all the black blood coming from His head. And perhaps Pigeon was smiling, Pigeon, perhaps he was, before he closed the curtains and the house was put out.

Pigeon is silent and patient while I stand here, holding it as if it's going to explode.

"It isn't mine," I say eventually, and pass it to him.

"No," he says. "It isn't."

Pigeon's holding the gun again now. It's lifeless. Dead.

"What can I do about all this?" I ask him my stupid question, here in the empty quarry, and stand, hopeless, waiting for the answer. Pigeon's answer. Pigeon's own. It doesn't come. He smiles just a bit, his eyes still that boy's eyes, the boy who had all those ideas and those stories which started this whole thing off, stories that'll go on and on as long as we're together, me and Pigeon, as long as it's never him or me, but both of us, together.

"How can I get back what you've lost?" I ask him again.

He's still smiling, just a bit. Considering. You can feel something building.

"Geiria," he says. *Words*.

He shrugs, his eyes searching the ground for them.

"Only words."

Alys Conran writes fiction, poetry, creative essays and literary translations. Previously, her short fiction has been placed in The Bristol Short Story Prize and The Manchester Fiction Prize. Her work is to be found in magazines including *The Manchester Review*, *Stand Magazine* and *The New Welsh Reader* and in anthologies by The Bristol Review of Books, Parthian Books and Honno Press. Having previously studied in Edinburgh and Barcelona, she completed her MA in Creative Writing at Manchester and then returned home to north Wales, developing projects there to increase access to creative writing and reading. She now lectures in Creative Writing at Bangor and is in receipt of an AHRC scholarship to write her second novel, about the legacy of the Raj in contemporary British life.

Acknowledgments:

Diolch o galon to Laura Ellen Joyce, Jodie Kim, Kathryn Pallant and Holly Ringland for our online living room of global conversations where Pigeon could breathe. Maia, for never letting me clip my wings even when I want to. And Joe, always, for a life with dreaming at its heart, food in its belly, and laughter snorting out of its nose.